ABBY'S TWIN

**Other books by
Ann M. Martin**

Leo the Magnificat
Rachel Parker, Kindergarten Show-off
Eleven Kids, One Summer
Ma and Pa Dracula
Yours Turly, Shirley
Ten Kids, No Pets
Slam Book
Just a Summer Romance
Missing Since Monday
With You and Without You
Me and Katie (the Pest)
Stage Fright
Inside Out
Bummer Summer

THE KIDS IN MS. COLMAN'S CLASS series
BABY-SITTERS LITTLE SISTER series
THE BABY-SITTERS CLUB mysteries
THE BABY-SITTERS CLUB series

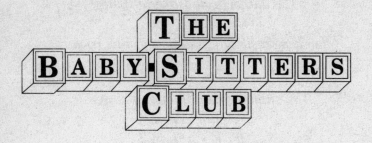

ABBY'S TWIN

Ann M. Martin

AN
APPLE
PAPERBACK

SCHOLASTIC INC.
New York Toronto London Auckland Sydney

The author would like to thank
Dr. Linda Gray
for her sensitive evaluation of this book.

The author gratefully acknowledges
Suzanne Weyn
for her help in
preparing this manuscript.

Cover art by Hodges Soileau

ISBN 0-590-69210-0

Copyright © 1997 by Ann M. Martin. All rights reserved. Published by Scholastic Inc. THE BABY-SITTERS CLUB, THE BABY-SITTERS CLUB logo, APPLE PAPERBACKS, and the APPLE PAPERBACKS logo are registered trademarks of Scholastic Inc.

12 11 10 9 8 7 6 5 4 3 2 1   7 8 9/9 0 1 2/0

Printed in the U.S.A.   40

First Scholastic printing, January 1997

CHAPTER 1

*T*aptaptaptap . . .

That was the sound of my short nails impatiently drumming on my desk. I didn't even realize I was doing it until my science teacher, Mrs. Gonzalez, turned and scowled at me.

You know the look. One of those real Looks of Doom teachers must learn in college. "Done with your test already, Ms. Stevenson?" she asked skeptically.

"Uh . . . yeah," I replied, taken by surprise. I'd been in sort of another world, happily remembering a soccer game I'd played in last year when I still lived on Long Island. I'd been the high scorer in that game. You should have seen me.

I'd probably started tapping the desk while I was picturing myself anxiously waiting for Maggie Sweeney to pass me the ball. She was completely boxed in, surrounded by players from the other team, and I was right out in the

1

open. Totally clear. What was taking her so long to figure it out? She had to know I was there. And then she did — pass the ball, that is. I slammed it right past the goalie. Score! Another point for Awesome Abby the Soccer Machine! "Yesss!"

"Perhaps you should use this extra time to check your answers," Mrs. Gonzalez suggested.

"Oh . . . yeah . . . okay," I agreed, looking down at my test. I squinted, frowned, and acted concerned. Actually, though, I wasn't even reading the test questions. I'm no science genius, but I'd studied, and I happened to know these answers. What was I supposed to do, rip my hair out and start sweating, worrying whether they were right or not?

Give me a break. Not my style.

While I pretended to agonize over my answers, I tried to return to my memories of that glorious, victorious soccer game. But it was like trying to reenter a fantastic dream after waking up in the middle of the night — almost impossible to do.

Don't get me wrong. It's not that I live in the past a lot. Not at all. It's just that I was bored. Actually, I was Bored.

It was January. I hate January. Hate. Loathe. Despise. February, too. The time between the holidays and springtime has got to be the longest, draggiest, most awful time of year.

It's also the time of year when my dad died in a car accident, which is probably another reason I detest the season so much.

That was four years ago. There I was, this incredibly sad nine-year-old kid, staring out the window at the bare, winter trees, wondering how such a rotten thing could have happened.

I remember that I didn't smile or even talk much after he died. Why bother? Then one day my best friend told me a joke, kind of a stupid joke, really. And I cracked up. Somehow, my laughter turned into tears. It was as though I were crying and laughing at the same time. Although it must have looked strange, it was actually a turning point. All the emotion I'd kept bottled up inside poured out that day. After that, I began to heal. Slowly.

Life went on, more or less. Of course, there was this gigantic hole in my life, where my father had been, but there wasn't anything I could do about it. The next big change came when my mother, my twin sister, Anna, and I moved here to Stoneybrook, Connecticut.

At first I was extremely bummed. I missed my Long Island friends. I thought I'd never find kids as great in Stoneybrook.

But it turns out that some of the Stoney-brook kids are actually cool. I made friends fast enough. Joining the BSC helped a lot. (BSC stands for Baby-sitters Club. I'll fill you in on that later.)

The sound of static filled the air, which meant that an announcement was about to come over the p.a. system. My classmates and I looked up expectantly from our papers.

"Eighth-grade classes have been canceled for the next two periods," said the distinctive voice of Mrs. Downey, the school secretary.

"All right!" I cheered.

Mrs. Gonzalez frowned.

"All eighth-graders are to report to the gymnasium for health checks," Mrs. Downey went on. "Seventh-graders will report during . . ."

I stopped listening. Health checks? What was this about? I raised my hand and Mrs. Gonzalez nodded at me. "What's the matter?" I asked. "Is there some plague going around or something?" (Anna and I had watched a scary movie the night before. It was about a killer virus that almost wiped out the planet.)

"No," Mrs. Gonzalez replied, smiling. "It's just routine. Eye tests. Hearing. And a scolio-sis check."

"A what?" I asked.

"Scoliosis check. For curvature of the spine."

I relaxed and settled into my chair as Mrs. Gonzalez began collecting the test papers. I already knew my eyes aren't great. That's why I wear glasses or contact lenses (depending on how I feel). I hear fine, and I stand up straight. No problems there.

If they'd been testing for allergies, that would have been a different story. Guess what I'm allergic to. Go ahead. Almost anything you'd answer would be correct. I'm allergic to . . . *everything!*

Well, not everything, but it seems that way sometimes. I'm sure if I landed on Mars I'd find some little Martian spore that would have me sniffling. The cosmos makes me sneeze.

Besides that, I also have asthma. I carry two inhalers, a regular one and a prescription one for really bad attacks. It's a drag, but it could be worse, right? I don't let it stop me from doing anything. And anyway, I'm stuck with it so there's no sense complaining.

When science let out, I left the classroom and was swept up in the river of eighth-graders flowing down to the gym. I felt glad to be missing my boring health class and happy to let the crowd carry me along until I was inside the gym.

Testing stations had been set up all around the gym. Teachers tried to create order, directing the kids into different lines, scolding them to keep the noise level down. At the different stations, people in white medical jackets had already begun the testing.

Craning my neck above the heads of other kids, I searched for Anna. It was kind of like looking for myself, except not exactly. Although Anna and I are identical twins, we don't look completely the same. Anna's curly brown hair is short and mine is long. We have the same narrow face, pointy features, and large brown eyes. And Anna wears glasses or contacts, just like me.

I didn't see her anywhere. Then I remembered that her orchestra group was on a field trip that day. Anna plays violin — *lives* to play violin — and she's a member of the Stoneybrook Middle School orchestra. (That's another difference between us. She's a musician and I'm an athlete.)

For a moment, I worried. Would she miss being checked?

It didn't really matter, though. As I mentioned, she already wears contacts or glasses. We know her hearing is fine — better than fine. All she has to do is hear a note to be able to play it. And I seriously doubted she had — what was it Mrs. Gonzalez had said? — scoliosis.

Across the gym I spotted a petite girl with a brown ponytail. I waved to her. It was Kristy Thomas, my neighbor and president of the BSC. Like me, she was waiting for her health check, standing in a crooked line of chattering kids. She noticed me and waved back. I'd see her after school on the bus and then again later at the BSC meeting.

When my turn came for the eye test, the short, blonde doctor (or nurse, or whatever she was) found my name on a computer printout, wrote down "corrective lenses," and sent me on to the next area.

A tall man in a white medical coat was sitting in front of some kind of electronic machine at a table. I had to put on headphones and tap either the right or the left one every time I heard a beep or boop in one of them. It was fun, like a game.

For the scoliosis test, I went to the girls' locker room. (*All* the girls did.) I lifted my shirt up as he indicated and stood with my arms at my sides while a slim, dark-haired woman ran her hand down my spine and poked at my shoulder blades. It tickled a little.

"I'm going to lift your hair up, all right?" the woman said. "I need to get a better look at your neck and shoulders."

"Sure," I agreed. I didn't remember having to do this at my old school. Maybe Anna and I'd been absent that day. Last year Mom had taken us out of school for a week to go to Disney World. Could my school have done the test then? Or maybe they simply didn't run tests at my old school. Anyway, this was a new one on me.

"Can you lower your right shoulder for me?" the woman asked.

I tried lowering it. "Is that good enough?" I asked.

Instead of answering, she made another request. "Breathe deeply and make your back as straight as you can."

I thought I *had* been standing straight, but I pulled in my stomach and tried to stand even straighter.

"Press your hands together and lean forward, please," the woman requested.

I did, and she ran her hand along my spine again. As I hung there, bent over, it suddenly occurred to me that I had seen only a few other kids leaning forward.

Maybe I just hadn't been paying attention.

"Okay, stand up," the woman said. "You can put your shirt back down." As I straightened, I noticed she was writing something on her printout. "Do you have any discomfort in your back?" she asked me.

"No. Never," I replied. Right about then, I started feeling alarmed.

8

"How about when you sit for a long time?"

"I never sit for long," I joked nervously as I tucked my shirt into my jeans.

The woman just kept looking at me expectantly.

"No, no pain," I answered seriously. What was going on?

She tore a piece of paper from her pad, signed it, folded it, stapled it, and handed it to me. "What's this?" I asked as I took it from her.

"It's a note for you to show your parents."

"What do you mean?" I asked, my voice climbing higher. "Do you think I have scoliosis?"

"I don't know for sure," she said calmly. "It's merely a recommendation that you have a more thorough exam."

"But I probably don't have it, right?"

"I'm not an orthopedist, Abby," she said, checking the printout on the clipboard for my name. "My job is to perform certain broad screening tests and recommend further testing if I think it's needed."

"Oh . . . well . . . I . . . no," I sputtered, too upset to talk clearly. "They can test all they want, but . . . but . . . I'm fine."

The woman glanced over my shoulder and I could tell she wanted to test the next person in line. In a daze, I moved away, out into the gym, my heart thundering like a race car engine.

Further testing. I didn't like the sound of that one bit.

CHAPTER 2

When I walked into BSC headquarters with Kristy Thomas, the only other person there was Claudia Kishi. She's almost always there first, because we hold our meetings in her bedroom. Claudia has long, silky, black hair and expressive, dark, almond-shaped eyes (she's Japanese-American).

Claudia is definitely cool. In fact, I'd say all my BSC pals rate high on my personal Abby Cool-Meter, but in very different ways.

For instance, Claudia scores a ten (on a scale of one to ten) for creativity. She's very artistic and very original. The wild outfits she wears are her own creations. That day she had on multicolored, tie-dyed painter's overalls she'd dyed herself over a blue, hand-beaded, long-sleeved shirt. Five colorful, bead-studded papier-mâché bracelets clattered softly on her wrist whenever she moved her arm.

I also give Claudia a ten for hospitality and

generosity. She supplies snacks for everybody, at every meeting, in her own, original way. As I sat down on Claudia's bed that day, something crunched beneath me. "Oops! Doritos!" Claudia giggled, as I leaned over and pulled a crushed bag of corn chips out from under the covers.

"You are too weird," I said with a laugh, handing them to her. Claudia is a total junk food freak, but her parents don't approve of her habit. That's why she stashes the stuff all over her room.

She hides books too — Nancy Drew mysteries. Claudia's parents don't approve of her passion for them, either. They don't think mysteries are intellectual enough. I guess that's because they're used to dealing with Claudia's older sister, Janine, who is an actual genius with a super-high IQ.

Claudia might be an artistic genius, but she's definitely not a school genius. In fact, she's had such a hard time in school that she's been bumped back to the seventh grade. I'd be mortified if that happened to me, but Claudia seems okay about it.

"Where is everybody?" Kristy complained from her seat in Claudia's director chair. (She always sits there.)

"It's not even five-thirty," I said, glancing at Claud's digital clock.

"It's five twenty-eight," Kristy countered, frowning. "They have exactly two minutes left."

Kristy and that clock! She demands that everyone arrive by the stroke of five-thirty. If you're even a minute late, you get the Look from Kristy. You know that expression, "If looks could kill . . ."? Kristy's Look probably could.

Kristy goes up and down the Cool-Meter. It goes up when she's being funny and smart and a great friend; it drops when she's being bossy, unbending, and crazed over her own club rules. (She sometimes makes the Cool-Meter seem like a roller coaster.)

I really like Kristy, but she makes me nuts, too. Anna suggested to me not long ago that my problem with Kristy is that we're both leaders who think we should be in charge, so we clash. I have to give that more thought. I suppose it's possible.

Kristy is petite and very athletic. She has brown hair and brown eyes. She doesn't do a thing to enhance her looks, which are already quite nice. A baseball cap, sweatshirt, and jeans are her usual attire. No makeup or jewelry.

Kristy is always herself and doesn't care what anyone thinks. I have to admire that. I'd say that no matter how I feel about her on a certain day she always rates an additional three points on the Cool-Meter for independence and self-reliance.

Also, I think it's extremely cool that even though Kristy's stepfather is a millionaire, Kristy is not the least bit stuck-up or snobby. Wealth doesn't matter at all to her.

She didn't start out rich. Just the opposite. Her father split right after Kristy's little brother was born. Their mother was on her own then, supporting four kids — Kristy's two older brothers (Charlie and Sam), Kristy, and her little brother (David Michael). Kristy's mom is a super go-getter, like Kristy, so the family did all right. But things became a whole lot easier for them once Watson Brewer came on the scene. He's the millionaire. When Kristy's mother married him, the Thomases moved across town to his mansion.

Kristy and I are neighbors, but her house is much fancier than ours. It's a lot noisier, too. Kristy's mom and Watson adopted a little girl from Vietnam, whom they named Emily Michelle. (She's two and a half now.) And Watson has two kids from his first marriage, Karen, who is seven, and Andrew, who is four. They spend every other month with their father. Sometimes there are seven kids in that house. Nannie, Kristy's grandmother, lives there, too. She helps take care of Emily

Michelle. With ten people going in different directions, Kristy's house can be a pretty hectic place.

"Five twenty-nine! Yesss!" Stacey McGill cheered as she hurried into the room. "Made it!"

Like Claudia, Stacey is a Cool-Meter ten. She's originally from Manhattan, which may be one reason why we click. Long Island is only a half hour from the city, and there's a lot of urban influence on Long Island style and personality (in my opinion, anyway).

Stacey landed here in Stoneybrook when her father's company transferred him to Connecticut. Just when Stacey was adjusting and making friends (she and Claudia had become *best* friends), her dad's company sent him back to the city. Saying good-bye was a bummer for her, but there was an even bigger, badder bummer waiting in Manhattan. That's where her parents decided they needed a divorce.

So, Stacey came back to Stoneybrook with her mother, and she joined the BSC again. She still goes back to New York on some weekends and stays with her father. It keeps her city sophistication sharp.

Stacey has blonde, permed hair, amazing big blue eyes, and happening clothes. But that's not why she rates. Style is what earns her a ten. By style I mean a way of being. Attitude. Maybe it's self-confidence. Stacey is just naturally cool. And you can tell that she hasn't been totally suburbanized yet. She still has "Manhattan" written all over her.

On the Cool-Meter I might even have to give Stacey extra bonus points for Coolness Under Stress. The stress in her case is diabetes. She has a very severe form of the disease and has to give herself insulin injections every day, plus watch her diet very carefully. She doesn't let her diabetes stop her from doing anything, though, and she's so upbeat most of the time that you'd never guess she was living with such a serious condition.

"It just now turned to five-thirty," Mary Anne Spier said, coming into the room and pointing to Claudia's clock. "I saw the numbers move."

"You're right," Kristy agreed.

Mary Anne smiled and sat down cross-legged on Claudia's bed.

My Cool-Meter registers major respect for Mary Anne. I'd have to call her personality Quiet Coolness. She doesn't talk a lot, but when she does she usually has something sensible to say. Plus, Mary Anne is an excellent listener. She really hears you. She's not just sitting there quietly daydreaming while you talk. (I've noticed that a lot of people tend to do that.) She's actually thinking about what you're saying. Big coolness points there.

Mary Anne is petite like Kristy, with large brown eyes and short brown hair. Her clothing is nice but kind of standard, not wildly fashionable or anything.

From what I hear, though, it's a real improvement over what Mary Anne had to wear until seventh grade: pigtails and little-girl clothes. That was her dad's rule back then, and Mary Anne had no mother to help convince her dad that she was growing up because her mother had died when Mary Anne was a baby. Ever since, her dad had tried to be super-parent. Her father's notion of excellent parenting was to have rules for everything. Strict rules.

But then . . . true love came to Mary Anne's rescue. True love for her father, that is. The former love of his life, Sharon Schafer, blew into Stoneybrook from California, just after she'd been divorced.

Her two kids blew into town on the same wind from the West Coast: Dawn and her younger brother, Jeff. (Actually, they arrived on a jet with their mother, but that doesn't sound nearly as poetic.)

Mary Anne and Dawn met at SMS (Stoney-brook Middle School, where most of us are students). They couldn't have looked more different. Dawn is tall and willowy, with long, white-blonde hair and a casual but trendy way of dressing. And there was little Mary Anne (she *is* short), still sporting pigtails and penny loafers. Despite this, they became instant friends. (Coolness points for Dawn, for looking beyond Mary Anne's clothes and hair.)

One day, while paging through Dawn's mother's old high school yearbook, Dawn and Mary Anne discovered that their parents had once been boyfriend and girlfriend. They instantly hatched a plan to get them back together. After all, Dawn and Mary Anne liked each other so much as friends, wouldn't it be even greater to be sisters?

So they thought. You know the saying, "Be careful what you wish for because you might get it"? Well . . . they got it. And it wasn't exactly the paradise they had had in mind.

Richard, Mary Anne's dad, and Sharon, Dawn's mom, married, and they all lived together in the old farmhouse Dawn's family had been living in, on Burnt Hill Road. (Jeff wasn't there anymore; he'd gone back to California to be with their dad.) I don't think blending two families is ever easy. In their case, it was complicated by several factors. One was food. Dawn and her mother adore health food. Mary Anne and her father aren't crazy about it. Sharon is sloppy. Richard is neat. Sharon couldn't stand Tigger, Mary Anne's kitten. And Mary Anne and Dawn overdid the sister thing at first. They started out in the same bedroom, and ended up in separate ones.

Before too long, though, the Schafer-Spier bunch had worked out most of the kinks and were chugging along as a pretty harmonious group. Richard was feeling so happy and secure that he took a good look at all his rules and let Mary Anne grow up. That's when she started dressing her age.

So anyway, things seemed to be working out for everyone. But then Dawn decided that she missed California and her dad too much. She decided to move back there full-time. Major trauma for Mary Anne, who'd grown incredibly close to Dawn.

Luckily, Mary Anne had her friends in the BSC. She and Kristy were still really tight. (They grew up as next-door neighbors.) And Mary Anne has a devoted boyfriend, Logan Bruno.

I suppose I could also give her coolness points for having a boyfriend. No one else in the group has a steady one. Stacey used to, but they broke up. Does having a boyfriend really have anything to do with being cool? I'm not entirely sure about that. I think being single and on your own is equally cool.

Anyway, Mary Anne has Logan and he's nice. He's down-to-earth, plays sports, and has an easygoing style. He's even a BSC member. (I hear he's great with kids.) He doesn't usually come to meetings, but if there is an overflow of work we call him. In BSC terminology, that means he's an associate member.

Our other associate, Shannon Kilbourne, lives near Kristy and me. Shannon's sweet and smart with piles of curly blonde hair. Her brains (she's in the Honor Society at her school) and her nice personality definitely rate high on the Abby Cool-Meter.

"Five thirty-one! Forgive us! Forgive us! We tried! Really!" A girl with thick, curly auburn hair threw herself to her knees in front of Kristy, her hands clasped together. Her glasses slid down her nose as she begged Kristy to give her a break. "I was walking Pow and he ran after a cat," Mallory Pike explained. "Jessi was with me."

"He waddled after the cat, really," amended Jessica (Jessi) Ramsey, the tall, dark-skinned girl who'd come sliding into the room along with Mallory. "Pow doesn't actually run."

Pow is Mallory's fat basset hound, and it's true, I've never seen him exactly speed anywhere.

"Waddled . . . whatever," Mallory conceded. "We still lost a minute going after them."

20

"Next time, start walking him a minute earlier," Kristy told them. "You can't plan on everything always going right."

"Okay, okay," Mallory said, settling down on the floor next to Jessi. Mallory and Jessi are best friends and, at eleven, are the youngest members of the club. (The rest of us are thirteen.)

Jessi's coolness comes from her natural elegance and the confident, graceful way she moves. She's studied ballet forever and she's super talented. Her dad takes her to ballet class in Stamford (that's the city nearest to Stoneybrook) every week.

Mal's coolness comes from her wit (the girl really whips off funny lines sometimes) and her talent as a writer and artist. Her goal is to be an author-illustrator of kids' books. Kids are something she certainly knows about since she's the oldest of eight.

"Let's start," Kristy opened the meeting. "I have something I want to talk to you all about. But first, does anybody have any new business to — "

She was cut short by the ringing of the phone.

Claudia was closest, so she snapped it up. "Baby-sitters Club. Oh, hello, Mrs. Papadakis."

Maybe this would be a good place to explain how the club works. We call it a club, but it's really more like a business. Kristy thought of it one day when her mother was making a zillion phone calls, trying to find a baby-sitter for Kristy's younger brother. It occurred to Kristy that it would be great if her mom could call one number and reach several qualified sitters. With that in mind, she rounded up her best friends and started the club.

We meet here every Monday, Wednesday, and Friday from five-thirty (sharp!) to six o'clock. Clients call us here to arrange baby-sitting jobs. (We meet here because Claudia has her own phone line, so we don't tie up anyone's family phone.) The person sitting nearest the phone answers, takes the information, and then says she'll call the client back. We decide who can take the job, then let the client know.

It sounds simple, but it takes some organization to make it run smoothly. That's why we each have jobs, or offices.

Kristy is president. She keeps things organized and comes up with the big ideas. One of her first ideas was that we should write down our baby-sitting experiences in a club notebook. Every time we go on a job, we have to write about it. The notebook becomes a resource for us. It's loaded with the most up-to-date information about our clients — who just started potty training, who's suddenly afraid of the dark, who's on a vegetable strike.

Claudia is vice-president. She's really more like a hospitality chairperson. As I said earlier, she provides her room, her phone, and plenty of snacks. She even makes sure there are always healthy snacks available for Stacey.

Stacey is treasurer, because she's so good at math. Her job consists mostly of collecting and keeping track of the dues we pay every week. Paying is a drag, but we need the money to help with Claudia's phone bill, to pay Charlie to drive Kristy and me to Claud's house, and to buy supplies.

One of the things we buy supplies for are our Kid-Kits (another Kristy idea). Kid-Kits are decorated cardboard boxes, filled with little toys, stickers, books, art supplies, and any other fun stuff we can think of. We sometimes bring them on sitting jobs, and they can really come in handy.

Mary Anne is our secretary. In my opinion, she has the most important job of all. She keeps track of the club record book, which holds our master schedules. After a client calls, Mary Anne consults the record book to see who's available to take the job. She records everybody's commitments there. For example, my soccer practices (during the season), my allergist appointments, and so on. If I make an appointment to have my hair trimmed, I tell

Mary Anne, and it goes into the book because it means I'm not available for baby-sitting at that time.

There's other important information in the book, too. It contains the addresses and phone numbers of all our steady clients. It tells us what we need to know about the kids (for example, special medications or special rules). It even lists how much each client pays.

Mary Anne is unbelievably organized. I don't think she has ever made a mistake. She's awesome, really. I couldn't do her job, that's for sure.

I might have to, though. Someday. That's because I'm the alternate officer. That means I have to learn everyone's job and be ready to jump in if anyone's sick or away or leaves the group.

So far I've been alternate president and alternate treasurer. (I didn't like being the treasurer, but I *did* enjoy being the president. I guess Anna is right. Maybe I am a take-charge type.)

Jessi and Mallory are called junior officers. They're not allowed to baby-sit at night (unless it's for their own siblings). The work they do in the afternoons and on weekends frees the rest of us to take night jobs, though.

So that's the club — who we are and how we work.

24

And, let me tell you, we were *working* at this meeting. No one got a chance to chat much because the phone never stopped ringing.

That was okay by me. I was kind of off in my own world. Scoliosisland, you might call it. I couldn't stop thinking about it. Was my spine really crooked? It couldn't be. It didn't feel crooked. I was an athlete, after all. How could I have a crooked spine?

That woman must have made a mistake. She had to have.

But what if she hadn't?

During the meeting, I nodded and smiled and went through the motions of being there. I even accepted a baby-sitting job. But all I could think of was scoliosis.

After awhile, I began to wish for a break in the phone calls. I wanted to talk about the health check. Had anyone else received a note? Did they know about scoliosis? Did they know anyone who had it? What would happen to me if I did have it?

There was no letup, though, and the time zoomed. Before I knew it, it was six. Everyone else was in a hurry to leave.

"Kristy," Mary Anne said, stopping at the door. "Wasn't there something you wanted to talk about?"

"I had an idea," she replied.

"Uh-oh," Claudia teased, laughing.

"An idea to sort of break up the winter blahs," Kristy continued. But she must have seen how eager everybody was to leave. "It can wait until the next meeting," she said.

That was all the permission everyone needed to hurry off to whatever else she had to do.

I wasn't as happy to leave. Without the distraction of the meeting I could worry about scoliosis full-time. And all I had to look forward to that evening was going home and breaking my news to Mom.

CHAPTER 3

"Abby, what's wrong?" Anna asked me the moment she walked through the front door. She set her violin case on the floor and stared hard at me. I sat slumped desolately on the couch, my legs sprawled in front of me. "What's happened? You look awful!" she said.

"You're lucky you went on a field trip today," I mumbled.

"It was really good," Anna said, her face brightening as she peeled off her parka. Then she frowned. "What's that have to do with anything?"

"Thanks to your trip, you didn't get . . . a note," I said ominously.

"A note?" Anna repeated in bewilderment. She pulled off her woolen hat and fluffed her hair. She'd just come from her violin lesson and was probably still thinking in terms of *musical* notes.

I was now dying to talk to someone about

this. All the way home Kristy and Charlie had yakked a mile a minute about the big basketball game coming up at Stoneybrook High. Charlie was psyched about it, and somehow it didn't seem appropriate to cut in and say, "Guess what? I may have scoliosis," so I kept my mouth shut.

"What kind of note do you mean?" Anna asked.

"A note — you know, a piece of paper with writing on it," I said, more irritably than I'd meant to. This whole thing was putting me in a horrible mood.

Just then, Mom came in the front door. In one gloved hand she clutched her worn, overstuffed briefcase. The *New York Times* was tucked under her other arm. "Wow! It's growing colder out there," she said with a shiver. In an instant, her sharp dark eyes darted between us, and she saw that something was up. "What's going on?" she asked.

I had the note clutched in my hand and I thrust it forward. "This!" I said. "This is what's going on."

Putting her briefcase and newspaper down on the coffee table, Mom took the note. She read it quickly, scowling in concern. "All right, well . . . we'll have you tested right away," she said calmly when she was done reading.

I couldn't believe she wasn't more upset

about this. She acted as though this were the same as having the car fixed or the boiler repaired. In fact, she'd been more upset the week before when the car started making a strange thumping noise. Maybe she hadn't read the whole thing. "Mom, did you — " I began.

"I got one too," Anna interrupted me.

My jaw dropped.

It didn't seem possible. How come she wasn't more upset?

Anna rummaged in her backpack and pulled out the note.

"But . . . but . . ." I stammered. "How? You weren't even there."

"They tested everybody in the orchestra at the end of school, when we got back from the trip," Anna explained. "Since we're twins, I guess it makes sense that we both have it," she added.

How could she be so calm?

Mom took off her coat and hung it up. "I'll have to ask around for someone to recommend a good orthopedist," she said, as if she were thinking out loud. "I'll call Dr. Hernandez. Perhaps he can recommend someone in the area. If I can't get a local recommendation, maybe we'll take you to someone in the city."

Mom is an editorial director at a big publishing house in New York City. She commutes every day. In many ways, she seems more comfortable in the city than here in Stoney-brook. She knows her way around better and knows more people there.

"Why aren't you guys more upset?" I cried, tossing my hands up in the air. "What does this mean? I never even heard of it before! What does it do to your back? How did this happen?"

Mom sat down next to me on the couch, and put her fingertips together thoughtfully. "I don't know a lot about it, Abby," she said. "I know it's not all that uncommon, and it's better to detect the problem when you're young, and that the treatment is usually successful."

"What's going to happen to us?" I asked anxiously. "What does treatment mean?"

"I'm not sure. Maybe you'll have to wear a brace," she replied.

"A brace!" I shrieked.

All I could envision was a horrifying image of myself sitting miserably with my head and arms sticking out of a sort of gleaming metal cage. Anna, too. We would clank together as we struggled to move.

Hot tears jumped to my eyes. "A brace!"

"Calm down, Abby," Mom said mildly. "I don't know what's going to happen. The note simply says to have you tested. So that's what we'll do. In the meantime, I'll try to track down some information so we can learn more about this."

"But we obviously have it," I said. "If just one of us received the note then . . . well . . . then maybe there would be a chance."

"We're not doomed," Anna said, shaking her head. "You're so overdramatic sometimes, Abby."

"Overdramatic!" I yelped. Honestly, sometimes I can't believe Anna is my twin. We are so *not* alike in some ways. "You just found out you might have scoliosis and you're not even upset," I pointed out. "I call *that* weird. Being upset is the normal reaction."

"Normal for you maybe," Anna countered.

"Yes, because I'm a normal person," I shot back.

"I'm normal," Anna said, sounding offended.

"Girls!" Mom interrupted sharply. "That's enough. You're both normal, just different."

The same but different. That's Anna and me exactly. We look alike, yet we don't dress alike or wear our hair alike. Our personalities are different, but sometimes we are the same in the strangest ways. (We both like the same movies, for example. Once we both bought my mother the exact same pair of earrings for her birthday without even discussing it. Things like that.)

And now, apparently, we were the same in a new way. We both had scoliosis.

I looked up at Anna, standing by the coffee table. Strangely enough, I realized I was almost glad she'd gotten a note too. It made me feel less alone.

She must have been feeling the same thing, because she said, "We'll get through it together, Abby. Don't worry."

I forced a little smile. "Okay, twin," I said. "You're right. We'll get through it together."

CHAPTER 4

"Any new business?" Kristy asked at our BSC meeting on Wednesday.

"I have some," I said. "I can't be here next Monday."

Kristy scowled. "Why not?" If you miss a meeting, Kristy expects you to have an extremely good reason.

I did.

"Anna and I have an appointment with an orthopedist in the city," I explained. "Dr. Hernandez recommended him. Normally you have to wait longer for a visit to this doctor, but he's seeing us as a favor to Dr. Hernandez. We have to go on Monday, because that's when he can squeeze us in."

"Why are you going to an orthopedist?" Stacey asked, sitting forward on Claudia's bed.

I'd been so confused by the note I hadn't even told my friends about it. Now, two days later, I felt calmer and I explained that Anna and I had received notes. "Did anyone else get one?" I asked.

My friends glanced at one another as they shook their heads. I was glad for them, but a little disappointed too. I wanted to think that a lot of kids had received the notes. If that were so, it would mean that the school was just being super cautious and there wasn't really anything to worry about.

Obviously, though, that wasn't the case.

"Well," I said with a sigh, "Anna and I did, so we have to check it out."

"Anna too, huh," said Jessi.

"Anna too," I said.

"Are you scared?" Mallory asked.

"Nah," I lied. I saw concern coupled with disbelief in Mal's eyes and realized there was no point in putting up a falsely brave front. These were my friends, after all. "A little, maybe," I admitted.

"I would be too," Mal said sympathetically.

"I knew a girl at my school in the city who had scoliosis," Stacey said. "It didn't seem like a big deal for her."

"Did she wear a brace?" I asked.

"I'm not sure."

"Couldn't you tell?" I asked incredulously.

"Not really."

"She probably didn't have one, then," I said.

34

How could a person wear a brace without anyone being able to tell? "Maybe she had surgery instead," I suggested glumly.

"Surgery!" Kristy cried. "What do you mean, surgery?"

"I just know that sometimes they treat scoliosis with surgery," I said. Mom, Anna, and I looked up scoliosis in the encyclopedia and that's what it had said.

"You probably won't need it," Mary Anne offered hopefully. "Not everyone with scoliosis has surgery."

I could see by the expressions on their faces that my friends were becoming worried. I didn't want to bring everyone down, so I forced a smile. "I'm sure it will all turn out okay," I said as cheerfully as I could.

The phone rang at that moment. Claudia answered. It was Mrs. Prezzioso needing a babysitter for Monday afternoon.

"Abby's not available," Mary Anne said as she wrote my orthopedist appointment into the record book. "Let's see who is."

After Kristy accepted the Prezzioso job, the phone rang again almost immediately. Mrs. Hill needed someone to sit for Norman and Sara.

I was glad for the break. It gave me the chance to calm myself. After Claudia said yes to the job with the Hills, there was a moment of quiet. "Do you want to talk some more?" Kristy asked me. "Or does it just upset you?"

"It's okay," I said. "I might as well face the facts."

"But you don't really have all the facts yet," Claudia pointed out.

"True," I admitted. "I'll tell you all more after we see the doctor on Monday."

"Okay, but if you need to . . . you know . . . talk, we're here," Stacey said.

"Thanks," I replied.

"Any other business?" Kristy asked. No one said anything. "I have some," she said. "Here's the idea I didn't have time to talk about at the last meeting. I've been noticing that the kids I've been sitting for seem really bored lately. Winter is just dragging on and on. What would you think of having a winter carnival?"

We all turned our heads toward the window, where fat snowflakes drifted past. So far it had been a very snowy winter and it wasn't showing any signs of stopping.

"What would we do at a winter carnival?" Jessi asked.

"We could do lots of stuff — winter stuff," Kristy said enthusiastically.

"Like have a snow sculpture contest?" Claudia suggested, her eyes brightening at the idea.

"Sure, and sled races," Kristy agreed.

"We could sell hot chocolate," Mallory added.

"I once saw a snowshoeing race in Central Park," Stacey said. "It was so funny."

Kristy smiled and nodded. "It would give everybody a lift, especially the kids. They really need it."

"*I* really need it," I said. "I'd love to do anything to take my mind off my curved spine. Count me in."

"Great," Kristy said.

"Count Anna in too," I said.

"Are you sure?" Kristy asked.

"Sure I'm sure. She needs something to take her mind off scoliosis too. She'll help."

"Terrific!" Kristy said. "Does everyone else want to do this? If we held it three weeks from this Saturday that should give us enough time. What do you think?"

A murmur of agreement filled the room. A winter carnival would certainly get rid of the winter blahs.

"One problem," Stacey spoke up. "We just restocked the Kid-Kits and there's not enough money left in the treasury for a special event. I mean, won't we need some supplies? Right off the top of my head I know we'll have to make posters or fliers to advertise and buy food for refreshments. We might need plywood to make booths."

Kristy folded her arms and settled into the chair. "Hmmmm," she murmured. I could almost see the idea wheels turning in her head. "How can we raise money?"

The room grew quiet as everyone started thinking.

"I could collect extra dues," Stacey suggested.

"Nooooo!" everyone said at once.

"How about a bake sale?" Mary Anne offered.

"We'd need money to buy baking supplies," Stacey reminded her.

"True," Mary Anne agreed glumly.

Kristy suddenly jumped up from her chair. She pointed toward the window with both hands. "There's our answer!" she cried. "Snow!"

"Uh . . ." I said, raising one eyebrow. "I don't think we can pay for supplies with snowballs. In the desert, maybe, but not in Stoneybrook."

Kristy laughed. "We'll shovel it! And we'll get our sitting charges to help us."

"Great idea!" cried Mallory.

"That is a good idea," I agreed. "You know what they say — there's no business like snow business."

Everyone groaned, then burst out laughing.

CHAPTER 5

monday

I thought shoveling snow to raise money was one of the most brilliant ideas I've ever come up with. Wrong! But how could I know? It seemed like a great way to make money, help out neighbors, and do something fun with the kids. It just goes to show that ideas that seem perfect in your head don't always turn out to be perfect in real life. Thank goodness we received a lucky break this morning.

The snow that fell during our Wednesday meeting didn't amount to much. It tapered off after covering everything with a fresh coat of white. On Thursday the temperature dropped to eleven degrees but no snow.

Kristy fretted about it through the entire Friday BSC meeting (while I silently fretted about my upcoming visit to the orthopedist). "How can we shovel snow when there's no snow?" she muttered, glowering out the window at the sky. "Come on, cooperate! Snow!" she commanded the heavy, gray clouds.

Wouldn't you know it! When Kristy says go, even the clouds jump to action.

Or so it seemed.

On Friday evening it started to snow after dinnertime. It kept coming, in fat white flakes, all through the night and into the morning. At eight o'clock Saturday morning, Kristy called me. "This is it!" she said excitedly over the phone. "Operation Snow Lift is on! Round up your kids and meet in front of my house at nine-thirty."

"But I'm not sitting for the Braddocks until ten," I told her.

"Well . . . call and ask if Haley and Matt can come out earlier. Mr. and Mrs. Braddock will probably be happy to get them outside."

"All right," I agreed.

When I phoned, Mr. Braddock answered, and — as Kristy had predicted — he was definitely amenable to the idea of Haley and Matt leaving the house earlier than planned. Apparently they were bouncing off the walls, dying to play in the snow. Mr. Braddock happily volunteered to drop them off at my house.

"Hi, guys," I greeted them when they showed up at my front door.

"Hi," said Haley, who is nine and has short blonde hair (with a long tail down her back) and big brown eyes.

I smiled at Matt and waved.

Matt, who is seven, is deaf. With a grin, he waved back.

Pulling on my jacket and grabbing my gloves, I went outside with the kids. I found a snow shovel in our garage, and we walked two houses down McLelland Road to Kristy's house. When we arrived, Kristy was already outside, bundled up and holding a snow shovel. Karen and Andrew were beside her, carrying kid-size snow shovels.

The Pike family's two station wagons pulled up to the curb. Mallory climbed out first. Behind her came her sisters: Margo (who is seven years old), Vanessa (who's nine), and Claire (five).

Eight-year-old Nicky and the ten-year-old triplets, Byron, Adam, and Jordan, were in the second car. Hidden under their scarves and hats, they were even harder to tell apart than usual. (Mallory says that once you get to know them it's a cinch to tell them apart. Being a twin myself, I know how that is, but still . . . the Pike triplets completely confuse me.)

The kids greeted each other excitedly, threw down their shovels, and immediately started bounding around in the knee-deep snow on Kristy's lawn.

Stacey's mother dropped her off, along with Charlotte Johanssen. Then Mr. Ramsey pulled up. Claudia climbed out of the car along with Jessi and her sister, Becca.

Charlotte and Becca greeted each other with hugs. (They're both eight and good friends.) Then they jumped onto the snowy lawn along with the others. In minutes Charlotte, Becca, Vanessa, Haley, Margo, and Claire were on their backs making snow angels.

"Look at all the long driveways around here!" Kristy exclaimed happily, spreading her arms wide at the glistening, snow-filled driveways that opened off the road for as far as we could see. Not one of them had been shoveled yet. "We'll make a fortune," she added. "It's so obvious, I don't know why I never thought of it before."

As she spoke, a small blue truck with a bright yellow snowplow at its front came barreling around the corner, the snow chains on its thick, oversize tires thunking loudly. It turned into Mrs. Porter's drive. (She lives in the house between Kristy's and mine.) The driver lowered the plow blade and began pushing away the snow.

"There's one potential client gone," Stacey noted glumly.

"Oh, so what? It's just one," Kristy scoffed. But I could see she was worried. If a lot of those snowplows showed up we'd be out of business before we started.

"Why don't we start with your driveway?" Mallory suggested to Kristy.

Kristy shook her head. "Charlie and Sam already have that job," she said. "It's one of their regular chores."

From the far end of the street, another snowplow truck came thunking down the block. It turned into my driveway. Kristy turned to me with questioning eyes.

"I forgot," I said. "After the last big snowfall, Mom called a snowplow guy whose number she saw tacked up in town. She told him to come do the drive next time it snowed."

"I hope everyone didn't do that," she muttered. "Come on, kids!" she called. "We've got snow to shovel."

The kids didn't hear her or pretended not to. They were having too much fun chasing one another, kicking up fluffy sprays of snow as they went.

"Snow shoveling time!" Kristy shouted again, casting an anxious glance at the snow-plow, which had already started clearing out my driveway.

Still no response.

Kristy put her fingers to her lips and whistled loudly. That caught the kids' attention. They turned and stared at her. "Come on. We came out to shovel snow, remember?" she said.

The kids gathered their shovels and we traipsed down McLelland. Kristy sang "Heigh-Ho" from Disney's *Snow White*, and we all joined in. (Except Matt, but he sensed the rhythm in everyone's movement and marched along.)

We felt good by the time we made our way up a long, snowy driveway and reached the front doorway of a big brick house. An elderly neighbor named Mr. Bendix answered, and I was sure he'd be glad to hire us. "Sorry," he said, though. "My son, Gerry, is on his way over right now to do it for me."

"No problem," Kristy said. "If Gerry wants some help, we'll be around."

Still singing "Heigh-Ho," we headed down the drive.

The trouble with this neighborhood (at least

in terms of snow shoveling) is that most of the houses sit at the end of long, sometimes steep, driveways. By the time we reached the next house, which belonged to the Kent family, I was panting a little. So was everyone else.

"I'm sorry, kids," Mrs. Kent there said. "I have a contract with a man who has a snow-plow. He'll be here to do my drive soon."

"Okay," Kristy said. "If he doesn't show up, we'll be around the neighborhood."

"Oh, I'm sure he'll show up," said Mrs. Kent, peering down the block. "I think that's his truck down there in the Stevensons' drive-way. He'll probably come to me next."

At Shannon Kilbourne's house Shannon was shoveling her driveway, along with her eleven-year-old sister, Tiffany, and her eight-year-old sister, Maria. They'd already completed the top half closest to their house.

Shannon waved when she saw us approaching with our shovels. "Hi, guys," she greeted us. "I have to help Mom at the school book fair so I can't go out with you to the other houses. But Mom says she'll pay us to do the driveway, so I figured I'd get started," she said. "Maria and Tiffany offered to help for free. All the money we earn can go to the Winter Carnival fund."

"All right!" cried Jessi.

We got to work shoveling the driveway.

With everyone working it went fast. In less than fifteen minutes we'd collected our money.

"See how easy it is?" Kristy said.

"Yeah, but we had Shannon and her sisters helping," Claudia pointed out.

Shannon wore an apologetic expression. "Sorry I can't help with the rest," she said. "I promised Mom a long time ago I'd help her at the school."

"No problem," Kristy assured her as we waved good-bye and headed down the driveway.

"We'll do fine even without them," Kristy said confidently, as she knocked on the next door. Mrs. Stellar, a short, dark-haired woman in a pink sweatsuit, answered. When we offered to shovel the walk, she smiled. "Super," she said. Then she frowned uncertainly. "The driveway is awfully long and steep. Are you children sure you can handle it?"

My friends and I exchanged glances. Was she calling *us* children?

"Sure," Kristy said. "We just did the Kilbournes' driveway."

"All right, then," Mrs. Stellar agreed. "The job is yours."

Everyone cheered and we set to work.

It only took about two minutes, though, before a shovelful of snow went flying past me. Looking up, I saw that Nicky, Matt, and the

Pike triplets were in the middle of a snow-throwing battle with Vanessa, Claire, Margo, Becca, Charlotte, and Haley.

"Hey, you're supposed to be working," Kristy scolded them, as a ball of snow landed on her hat.

"But shoveling is boring," Vanessa protested.

"And my shoulder hurts," Haley added.

"It's not boring, it's fun," Kristy said brightly. "Hey, let's sing 'Whistle While You Work'!"

"Enough with the *Snow White* songs, already," said Byron.

Kristy made a face at him as she lifted her shovel. "Come on, back to work," she said firmly.

We dug in again, but when I looked up a few moments later, I noticed that all the kids were gone. They'd begun building a snow elephant on the woman's lawn. "Uh, guys," I said to my friends. "We've lost our workforce."

"Oh, well," said Claudia, laughing. "We might as well just do it ourselves."

We returned to work, keeping an eye on the kids as we did. Mrs. Stellar had been right. The driveway was hard to shovel. The snow felt heavier with every shovelful I lifted.

By the time the job was done, my back and shoulders ached. Kristy went back to the

47

house to collect our money and returned with a disgusted expression on her face. "This is all she gave me," she said, holding out two five-dollar bills. "She said, 'You children go buy yourselves some hot chocolate.' "

"Ten dollars," Stacey moaned.

"She was going to give me five, but she threw in the extra five when she saw the snow elephant," Kristy added with a grin. "She thought it was adorable."

"Did you tell her it wasn't enough?" Claudia asked.

"I couldn't. She closed the door too fast," Kristy said, shoving the bills into her jacket pocket. "For the next job, we'll have to settle on a price and state it up front."

The next job? I thought miserably. I was already sore. The idea of a next job wasn't too appealing.

"Byron put snow down my neck!" Margo complained to Mallory, her teeth chattering. She was covered in snow from head to foot.

"Mallory, stop them!" Vanessa squealed. The triplets ran after her, each carrying a big chunk of snow.

"Cut it out!" Mallory shouted at them, but they paid no attention.

All the kids were red-faced and snowy. "Maybe we should call it quits," Claudia suggested.

"Quits?" Kristy said in a shocked voice. Then she looked down the block at the three small plows working in three different driveways. "Maybe you're right," she told Claudia.

We gathered the kids and headed back to Kristy's house. The kids were soaked and glad to take off their wet things. We draped all the icy scarves, hats, and mittens in the mudroom. They made little puddles as they dripped onto the floor.

"Well, this was a dud idea!" Kristy said as she unceremoniously tossed the money we'd earned onto the kitchen table.

"It's not enough, but it's a start," Stacey said, smoothing the crumpled bills. "At least it gives us money to make advertising posters or have fliers printed."

Kristy took a gallon of milk from the fridge and poured it into a pot. "What's the sense in advertising if we don't have money to hold the carnival?"

She certainly had a point. And I could see she was disappointed that her winter carnival idea might not happen. So was I. It sounded fun.

Maybe we were simply tired from shoveling, but no one said much after that. We served the kids hot chocolate in the den, played a game of charades with them, and then, pretty soon, it was time for them to go home.

On Sunday I was sore from shoveling. I wondered if my friends felt the same. Or was I more sore because I had scoliosis? Could they have shoveled several more drives without feeling it?

Anna was especially quiet and seemed tense. We watched TV together but didn't talk much. I could tell Anna was as worried about our upcoming appointment with the orthopedist as I was.

The weather outside seemed to mirror our mood. Fat, gray clouds hung low in the sky, as if they too were waiting for something.

On Monday morning, though, the waiting ended. Things started happening.

The first thing that happened was snow. Lots and lots of it. When Anna and I came down to breakfast, we saw that the entire world was blanketed in white, about five inches thick. It had happened during the night. "Snow day!" I said with a smile. "Bet you!"

Mom was still in bed. She'd taken a rare day off so we could go to the orthopedist at three o'clock.

Anna snapped on the kitchen clock radio, which was set to the local station. "Stoneybrook Day School, Stoneybrook Academy and all Stoneybrook public schools, all canceled."

I yawned and stretched contentedly. "It's back to bed for me."

But as I headed out of the kitchen, the phone rang. "Hello?" I said, yawning into the phone.

"It's me. Come over to my house as fast as you can." It was Kristy. "I just had a great idea."

I rolled my eyes. "I was on my way back to bed."

"See you in five minutes," she said, hanging up.

Anna gazed at me with questioning eyes. "Kristy's had a great idea," I informed her.

"Too bad," Anna said as she headed out of the kitchen.

I dressed quickly, then grabbed a Pop-Tart and went to the closet for my coat. I was curious to find out what Kristy had in mind.

When I reached her house, Kristy and Shannon were already outside, knocking snow from the windows of Charlie's car with long-handled snow brushes. The engine was running. "What's up?" I asked.

"Charlie is taking us over to Bradford Court," Kristy said. "We're going to make a fortune cleaning off cars. School is canceled, but most people still have to go to work."

As Charlie drove along, Kristy explained why it would be better to work in Claudia's neighborhood. "The houses are much closer together, so there are more of them and we don't have to walk as far. And the driveways aren't all that long, so hardly anybody has a contract with a snowplower," she explained. "I should have thought of it Saturday."

She was absolutely right. Charlie let us off in front of Claudia's house. Claudia and Stacey were already working on Mrs. Kishi's car. Stacey was scraping ice from the windshield, while Claudia shoveled behind the car. "Mom has to go in to the library today," Claudia said. (Her mother is head librarian at the Stoneybrook Public Library.) "She paid us to shovel her out, and we're almost done."

Jessi and Mallory waved from the driveway next door. They were working on another car.

Mary Anne's father dropped her off in front of the house, and in minutes we'd all landed jobs cleaning off cars. It was easy. As people came outside to work on their cars, we offered to do it for them. They were happy to accept. We didn't even have to knock on doors.

In two hours we'd made a lot of money. People paid us very generously. "All right!" Kristy cheered as she counted the bills. "Winter carnival, here we come!"

I checked my watch. It was time for me to go home. *Orthopedist, here I come*, I thought, with a whole lot less enthusiasm.

CHAPTER 6

By four o'clock that afternoon, Anna and I were sitting in Dr. Abrams's office with Mom, waiting for him to come in to speak to us. After he repeated the same scoliosis checks we'd gone through in school, his assistant had X rayed us in a room down the hall. Dr. Abrams was taking forever to examine the results.

I was a wreck.

"Do you think it's a good thing or a bad thing that this is taking so long?" I asked anxiously. "I mean, if there was nothing really interesting to see, he would be here by now, wouldn't he? Maybe not, though. Maybe our bones are so boring he fell asleep."

"He does have to look at two sets of X rays," Mom reminded me.

"That's true," I said, jiggling my foot nervously. "I guess it takes twice as long. But two times nothing is still nothing. If there was nothing to see, he should be here in the same amount of time as if there was only one nothing to see . . . shouldn't he? I mean, mathematically that makes sense."

Mom smiled at me indulgently.

Anna seemed intent on examining the knitted hem band at the bottom of her sweater. She wasn't even listening to me.

"Don't you think he should be here by now?" I prodded Anna.

"I guess," she murmured, her fingers working along the hem. "I don't know."

Of course, I didn't know, either, but this waiting was making me insane. I wished Anna would say something. At least I'd have someone to talk to. "If he doesn't come in soon, I'm paging him." I got up and lifted the receiver of his desk phone. "Hello, doctor," I spoke into the phone in my best Groucho Marx voice, "where are you? I've got two girls with crooked backs. They look like the Twin Towers of Pisa. Come quick!"

At that moment, the door opened and Dr. Abrams came in holding a manila file folder in his hands. He was a short man with only a ring of dark hair around his head. He had a nice smile and a friendly face.

Embarrassed to be caught hovering over his phone, I leaped back into my seat. "I was about to send a search party out to find you," I joked nervously.

Anna rolled her eyes as she slumped in her seat. I just shrugged quickly.

"Sorry to keep you waiting," Dr. Abrams said, seating himself behind his desk and opening the folder. "Measuring spinal curves is a bit time consuming. I have to be very precise." He glanced down at his notes. "Which one of you is Abby?"

Instantly, I felt ice cold. My mouth was as dry as sand. "Me," I croaked.

Dr. Abrams sat back in his chair. "The word 'scoliosis' comes from a Greek word, meaning 'crooked,' " he said.

Skip the history lesson and get to the point, I thought.

"It's not uncommon for a spine to be somewhat curved. It's a matter of degree, though. You have a definite curve in your spine," he said slowly, carefully, as if he were considering every word. "But the curve is at about a fourteen-degree angle, which is less than twenty. We don't usually treat an angle that is less than twenty degrees."

I barely dared to breathe. I had no idea what he was talking about.

"Which means what, exactly?" Mom asked.

"Practically, it means that the amount of curvature in the spine probably will not progress and that it won't present a problem in the future," he replied. He held up my X ray and used his pencil to point out my spine and its curve. It didn't look *that* crooked to me, but it was hard for me to tell what I was looking at.

"Yesss!" I cheered, pumping my fist in the air. What a relief! No problem. Exactly what I'd hoped to hear. "Anna, we're okay," I said, smiling at her.

She didn't return my smile. "What about me?" she asked, turning her attention to Dr. Abrams.

The doctor sighed and sat forward. He drummed his fingertips on the folder a moment before speaking.

All my happy excitement drained away.

"It's about twenty-five degrees, Anna," he said. "I've seen much more severe curves. You're also less skeletally mature than Abby. Your bones are not quite as fully developed. While hers are almost finished growing, yours aren't. That means the curve I'm seeing in your spine now is likely to worsen, if left untreated."

Mom took Anna's hand in hers. "What do we do?" she asked.

"You'll have Anna fitted for a brace."

"A brace!" I gasped without meaning to.

"It's really not as bad as it sounds," Dr.

Abrams said. "Anna's curve is low. She probably won't need a full Milwaukee brace."

He opened a thick book on his desk and showed us a picture of a girl in a brace with metal rods up the front and back, and a ring around her neck. It looked so confining. I remembered the cage I had imagined.

Dr. Abrams flipped to another page. The girl in this picture wore a much smaller brace. It looked more like a thick belt, going from under the armpit on one side to lower on her rib cage on the other. It wrapped around the girl's waist and was held together by three Velcro straps.

It didn't exactly look like a load of laughs, either, but there was a lot less to it than the Milwaukee thing.

"This is a low-profile brace," Dr. Abrams explained. "I think this will be enough for Anna, especially since her curve is located in the lower lumbar area of her back."

"What do you mean, *you think*?" Mom asked.

"I'd like to have Dr. Sherman look at it," he replied. "She's an orthopedist and her office actually makes the brace. I don't do that. Each brace has to be individually fitted. I'm going to make a recommendation for a low-profile brace, but it's really up to Dr. Sherman." He wrote on a prescription pad and handed the sheet across the desk to Mom. "My nurse will give you Dr. Sherman's card. Call her right away, because it's not easy to get an appointment." He reached into his top drawer and handed Mom some pamphlets. "These should answer more of your questions."

"Thank you, doctor," Mom said, putting the paper and pamphlets in her purse.

"Anna," Dr. Abrams began, "don't let this upset you. You won't be wearing the brace for the rest of your life. It's lucky that we caught this problem now, while your bones are still developing. We can stop it from progressing."

Anna forced a weak smile as she rose from her chair. She'd become extremely pale. Her eyes were red, as if she might cry. I felt like crying for her.

Out in the hall, I put my hand on her shoulder. "Sorry, Anna," I said.

"Why are *you* sorry?" she asked.

"I'm sorry that . . . I don't know . . . that you have to go through all this."

"It's not your fault," she said in a small voice.

Of course it wasn't my fault. So why did I feel like it was? Maybe I felt guilty that I'd been given the good report and Anna hadn't. We were twins, after all. Shouldn't we go through something like this together?

"Don't worry," I told Anna as we walked

down the hall. "I'll be with you on this one hundred percent. You can count on me." Right then and there I promised myself I was going to be the best, the most supportive, caring, helpful twin possible.

CHAPTER 7

On Tuesday we had my favorite kind of snow day — you know, the kind that starts off with enough ferociously falling snow to close things down, which then tapers off immediately after they've announced school is closed. That way you have the day off but you're not stuck inside.

Once again, the BSC made a bundle of money cleaning off cars and helping people dig out of their driveways. Kristy had invested some of our Monday earnings in five cans of this spray stuff that instantly melts ice off windshields. It was a huge help and enabled us to work even faster than before. (While I worked on a car one morning I had the idea that BSC could also stand for Beat the Snow Club.)

Kristy, Claudia, and I were working on Mrs. McGill's car while Stacey counted our earnings. (Jessi, Mallory, and Mary Anne were working on a car across the street.) As we worked, I told them about Anna's and my visit to the orthopedist.

"Is Anna very upset?" Claudia asked, knocking snow from her brush.

"Yes. She handles things much more quietly than I do," I replied. "But I'd say she's pretty upset."

Stacey finished counting the money. "We can definitely afford to hold the carnival now," she reported happily, packing the bills into a neat pile.

"We might as well work on it today," Kristy said as she spritzed the side mirror with the ice melting stuff. "After all, it's a free day off. If only we could make it to the mall to shop for supplies."

"I can ask Mom if she'll drive us out there," Stacey suggested. "Bellair's is opening late today because of the snow, so maybe she won't mind taking us to the mall before she goes to work." (Mrs. McGill is a buyer for Bellair's department store downtown.) Stacey ran inside to ask her mother, then return to report that Mrs. McGill had agreed.

We all went inside Stacey's house to call home for permission to go out to the mall. I didn't really have to call, because Mom had braved the storm and taken the train into work. When she's at the office Anna and I don't have to call to ask about every little thing. She just expects us to use good judgment.

I wanted to check in with Anna, though. I was worried about her. "Why don't you come with us?" I suggested.

"No, thank you," she replied in a dull voice. "I'm going to stay in and read some of the books Mom brought home about scoliosis."

"I'll come home then," I offered.

"No, don't. You'll just distract me while I'm trying to read."

"Are you sure?"

"Positive."

"All right, if you're sure." I hung up, still not feeling right about things. Running around with my friends the day after Anna had received the news about her scoliosis wasn't exactly being supportive. But if she'd rather stay home and read, what could I do?

We didn't all fit into Mrs. McGill's car, so Jessi called her dad, who was also going into work late because of the snow. He agreed to drive out to the mall too.

We met up again in front of the big fountain in the middle of the mall. (It's so cool. It sprays pink water!) "To make the most of our time, we should split into groups and meet back here in an hour," Kristy suggested. "The first thing we need to do is decide how to advertise. I think fliers would be better than posters. With fliers people can put them up at home and keep the information. Claudia and Mallory, why don't you be in charge of those."

"Okay," Claudia agreed. "We can go to Artist's Exchange for special paper and a couple of markers. That won't cost too much."

Stacey handed Mallory some money, then she and Claudia went off to the art supply store. "See if you can find some decoration stuff, too." Kristy called after them as they headed for the escalator.

"Okay," Claudia called back.

"They've started selling awesome hot chocolate mixes at Just Desserts," Mary Anne said. "Sharon brought home a can of mint chocolate the other night. She said they have lots of different kinds."

"Good idea," Kristy said. "But are they expensive?"

"I don't know," Mary Anne admitted. "I suppose it would be cheaper in the supermarket, but this hot chocolate was the best I've ever had."

"We could always charge a few cents extra for it," Stacey pointed out. "If it's really great, people will pay."

"It's great, trust me," Mary Anne said.

We sent Mary Anne and Jessi off with twenty dollars to see how much hot chocolate they could buy. "What else do we need?" Kristy mused.

"Well, on the way over we were talking about having sled rides," Stacey recalled. "But we were afraid sleds with sharp runners might be dangerous. Why don't we go to Toy Town and see if they have any inexpensive plastic ones?"

So Stacey, Kristy, and I did that. It turned out that we could afford three of them. We also found a funky art set with squirt bottles and paint (kind of like food coloring) that you spray on the snow to make pictures. We bought two sets for the carnival.

When we met again at the fountain, Mary Anne and Jessi had four large cans of hot chocolate powder, all in slightly different flavors. Claudia and Mal were loaded down with bags. "What's all this sparkly stuff?" Kristy asked, peeking into one of the bags.

"Claudia had the best idea," Mal began.

"I thought we could make crowns," Claudia explained. "Snow Queen. Snow King. Snow Princess and Prince."

"The kids will like that," Stacey agreed.

Claudia opened another bag, revealing colorful metallic paper. "Isn't this beautiful?" she said excitedly.

"It's really nice, but what do we do with it?" Kristy asked.

"We can cut out snowflakes," Claudia said. "We can either sell them or have a booth where people cut out their own designs. It's not hard."

"That's a pretty *flake*-y idea," I said with a grin.

Everyone handed Stacey their change. She totaled it and looked up with a smile. "I think we have enough left for lunch at Friendly's as long as no one goes too wild."

This announcement was met with lots of cheering. As we headed toward Friendly's, I realized I was having a great time. Spending the day with my friends had put me in a terrific mood. I'd felt crummy ever since the health check last Monday. It was a relief to smile and laugh again.

But then I pictured Anna — home alone, probably playing some darkly melodic, heartbreaking piece on her violin.

How could I be *here* having so much fun when she was *there* feeling so rotten? I knew that it was her choice, but it still didn't seem right.

I should have gone home despite what she'd said. She'd done the noble, unselfish thing by telling me to go.

I, on the other hand, had done the selfish thing by listening to her and actually going.

I suddenly saw that very clearly.

"What's the matter?" Mary Anne asked me when we reached the entrance to Friendly's. "You look so worried."

"I shouldn't be here today. Not now, when Anna needs me so much," I said guiltily.

Mary Anne nodded sympathetically. "You could bring her a piece of cake or something. At least it would show you were thinking of her."

"Piece of cake," I joked, appreciating the suggestion. But I knew a treat wouldn't make up for my thoughtlessness. I felt so guilty. From now on I'd have to realize that everything was going to be different. I would have to spend a lot more time with Anna, whether she said she wanted me to or not.

CHAPTER 8

"So, Anna, what do you want to do?" I asked the moment I returned home that afternoon. Anna was sitting on the couch in the living room. A pile of books was beside her, and she was watching some orchestra on the educational public station. I figured *that* couldn't be a whole lot of fun. She needed to do something exciting.

"You're standing in front of the TV," she said.

"Sorry," I apologized, stepping aside. "But it's not like anyone is actually *doing* anything you're going to miss."

"They *are* doing something," Anna said. "They're playing music and I want to watch them."

I studied the set. Rows and rows of people dressed in dull, formal outfits, wearing serious expressions, and playing slow, gloomy music.

Okay, so — technically — they were moving. But barely.

How could she stand to watch this? It was so boring.

And the music was so sad. Anna was probably just sitting there brooding about her scoliosis. I needed to snap her out of her sad, self-pitying state.

"I know!" I cried. "I borrowed that new video game from Kristy, Drag Race Canyon." It was a great game. Super graphics. I really felt as if I were careening around a mountainous road in a race car. It was exciting — just the thing to take Anna's mind off her problems.

I took the video cartridge from my jacket pocket and then switched the TV to channel three.

"Hey!" Anna cried indignantly.

"You'll love this game," I assured her as I popped the cartridge into the game system. "Do you want to be the yellow car or the green?"

"I want to watch the concert, Abby. I was enjoying it!"

"Okay, you be yellow," I said. I handed her a control pad. "The thing is to slow down just a little on the curves. If you go too slow, you lose time. If you go too fast you spin right off the course and crash into stuff."

"Abby, did you hear what I said?" Anna asked.

"What? Are you saying you'd rather sit around and mope than play an exciting game with me?"

"I wasn't moping," she muttered.

"Sure you were. I mean, you have a perfect right to be bummed. But it's not going to help anything."

Anna sighed deeply. "Okay. I still don't think you're listening. But if it will make you happy . . ."

I smiled, pleased. It was my first victory in cheering up Anna. I'd roused her from her sullen state, and now we were doing something fun. Together. It made up for my selfishness in running off to the mall with my friends this morning. I felt a whole lot less guilty.

Sitting cross-legged in front of the TV, we played the game. I have to say Anna was hopeless at it. Every two minutes she was either crashing or stalling out. "Concentrate," I told her.

"I don't like video games," she replied.

"You're just not used to them."

"No, I don't like them."

"Everyone likes them," I insisted. "If you keep practicing, you'll get the hang of it."

"Abby, I don't want to do this, okay?" Anna said, a sharp edge in her voice.

I snapped off the game. "Okay." I cast around in my mind for something else we could do. "Want to look through this together?" I suggested, picking up a glossy catalog that had just come in the mail. I handed it to Anna. "We can circle stuff we'd like. Remember how we used to do that when the toy catalogs came around the holidays?"

Anna smiled. "I remember," she said fondly. "You always circled the outrageous stuff — the kid-size sports car, the life-size gorilla." She laughed softly and seemed to have already cheered up. But when she looked at what I'd handed her, she wrinkled her nose with distaste. "*Workout Wear?*"

"Yeah, really cool sports clothes," I said. "We're not really going to send for them. We'll just have fun picking them out."

Anna and I sat together on the couch. "Great bike shorts," I said, pointing to a pair in neon purple.

"I guess," Anna said. "They'd look really nice on you."

"What do you like on this page?" I asked.

"Nothing, really. You know I'm not much for sports."

"It's never too late to start," I countered. "I know! We can pick out twin workout wear."

"Twin clothes!" she cried.

"Let's start," I suggested. "We are twins after all."

"I guess we're not as twin as we used to be," Anna said quietly, flipping the page of the sports catalog.

I felt as if I'd been slapped.

Not as twin? "What . . . do you mean?" I asked weakly.

Anna looked up at me. "Well, I'll be wearing a brace, and you won't. No one will have trouble telling us apart now."

To be honest, everyone can tell us apart now. Our haircuts are completely different, for one thing. But we do look alike. I guess we still might be confusing to some people.

Anna was right, though. The brace might really set us clearly apart.

I wasn't exactly thrilled by that idea.

I like being a twin. I love it, in fact. No matter how different Anna and I are, we're twins. It's as simple as that. There's this twin bond between us that I've always taken for granted. When you're a twin, you're indescribably close to another person. You always feel confident that no matter what happens, you're never alone.

Suddenly — maybe for the first time ever — I felt very alone.

It was a horrible feeling.

Anna had said the words as if it didn't matter to her one bit. How could she be so cold about it? Didn't the idea of not being twins as much as before hurt her the way it hurt me?

Then it struck me! She meant to hurt me. Why? Maybe because she was jealous.

It was an awful thought, but it made perfect sense to me. Anna was probably jealous because she was going to have to wear a brace and I wasn't.

I flipped the catalog shut. "Who cares about these stupid clothes," I said.

"You do," Anna replied.

"Not really. What I care about is you, helping you through this. I'm coming with you to see that other doctor."

"You don't have to," Anna objected.

"Yes, I do. We're twins, aren't we? We help each other out. We do stuff together."

"We're not getting a brace together."

How could I argue with that? Believe it or not, I tried.

"I'd wear one too if I could," I said.

Anna laughed. It sounded scornful and harsh to me.

"I would. I know — I'll wear yours sometimes so I know exactly what you're going through."

"You can't. The brace will be made from a mold of my body. It won't fit you."

"Yes, it will," I insisted. "We're twins. Remember?"

"I need a brace and you don't," Anna countered, standing up and walking toward the stairs. "Remember?"

CHAPTER 9

wednesday

I am so exited about the carnivul. Today I had this grate idea to get redy for it. It reely worked out. But not at all in the way I exspected.

when you sit for the Barrett — DeWitt kids, nothing ever seems to turn out as you expect it to!

At our Wednesday meeting everyone came in chatting enthusiastically about Claudia's great idea. We knew about it before we read what she wrote in the club notebook, because we'd walked right past it on our way in.

"Very cool," Kristy said as she took her seat. "Awesome advertisement, Claudia."

"Thanks, but I had help," Claudia replied as she worked on a sketch for the Winter Carnival flier she was designing.

"The Stacey look-alike out there is unbelievable," Mallory added.

Here's what happened. Claudia was very excited about the snow sculpture contest we were planning for the carnival. But she worried that the kids wouldn't really know how to make the sculptures. So that afternoon she decided to have a practice session.

She and Stacey were scheduled to sit for the Barrett-DeWitt kids that afternoon. They'd teamed up because there were so many kids to sit for. It's a club rule that we send more than one sitter when there's a big group of kids.

Mrs. Barrett has three kids from her first marriage — Buddy, who's eight; Suzi, five; and Marnie, two. Recently, she married Franklin DeWitt, who has four kids from his first marriage — Lindsey, who's eight; Taylor, six; Madeleine, four; and Ryan, two.

Having such a large group of kids made Claudia think it would be a terrific testing situation for the snow sculpture contest. (I suspect our snow shoveling fiasco had reminded her that great ideas don't always go the way you expect, especially where kids are concerned.)

"Okay, guys," Claudia announced. "I'm going to show you how to make a snow sculpture."

"Yay! A snowman!" Suzi cheered.

"Like a snowman, but not exactly," Claudia said.

"A snow lady?" Lindsey asked.

"It could be. Or it could be a cat or a dog or a dragon. Anything you like."

"Make Stacey!" Ryan suggested.

"Oh, that's too hard," Stacey objected.

"No, it's not," Claudia said, excited by the artistic challenge. "I bet I could do it. Let's start by rolling up snowballs for the body."

The kids jumped right to it but soon grew tired of rolling their balls and began throwing them at one another. After a brief snowball fight, Stacey and Claudia managed to direct them back to the snow sculpture. (Most went back, anyway. Marnie was content to keep digging in the snow with her small plastic shovel.)

Soon they'd built a figure about five feet high. "There's your body, Stacey," Claudia announced.

"I'd better start exercising." Stacey laughed. "If that's my body, I'm looking pretty lumpy."

Claudia giggled. "This is just the beginning, the basic form. Once you have your form built, you can start smoothing and sculpting."

"How do you do that?" Taylor asked.

"Lots of ways," Claudia told him. "You can use a stick or a shovel. I like to use my hands." She smoothed the bumpy snow with the edges of her gloved hands. "See? I'm making shoulders and forming arms."

"Cool," said Lindsey. "Can I help?"

"Sure," Claudia replied, still working.

"I'll help, too," said Stacey.

"No, you can't. You have to model," Claudia told her.

Claudia was soon so engrossed in her Stacey snow sculpture that she forgot about the kids. She figured they were there watching her, and she could see that Stacey was watching them.

Stacey *was* keeping her eyes on them, but after awhile the kids weren't watching Claudia anymore.

"Can we make our own snow sculpture?" Buddy had quietly asked Stacey.

Stacey nodded, taking care not to move her

head too much. She'd posed for Claudia before and knew that Claud insisted on a steady, unmoving model.

It wasn't long before Claudia had created a remarkably lifelike snow sculpture with an amazing resemblance to Stacey. She stepped back to study it and smiled, pleased with the result. "Wow! That came out even better than I expected," she said. "Too bad it's going to melt."

Claudia noticed a gleam of laughter in Stacey's blue eyes. "What's so funny?" she asked, perplexed.

"You'd better not take another step backwards," Stacey replied mischievously. "You might get bitten."

Claudia whirled around and shrieked in surprise.

The kids burst into peals of laughter.

A four-foot-high snow dragon stood behind Claudia, its jaw open as if about to bite.

Claudia had been so caught up in her work — especially once she came to the sculpting of Stacey's face — that she hadn't noticed the kids quietly working on the dragon. "It's good!" she cried sincerely. "Really good!"

The dragon looked like a sea serpent, with part of its body underground and part of it rising in snowy humps, ending in a spiky tail resting on the ground. The kids had found evergreen branches under a nearby tree and placed them along the dragon's spine for decoration. Two large, glistening rocks made eyes.

"Our dragon looks like it's trying to bite your Stacey," Suzi giggled.

Claudia realized she was right. It did look that way.

People walking along the sidewalk stopped to admire both sculptures. "That is so creative," said a woman with two small children.

"You'll see more of these at our winter carnival," Claudia informed her. "You should come and bring your friends."

"Oh, really?" the woman said, interested. "When is it?"

"Two weeks from this Saturday. Over on Burnt Hill Road," Stacey said. (We'd decided to hold the carnival at Mary Anne's house.)

"Where can I find more information?" the woman asked.

"We'll be handing out fliers soon," Claudia told her.

"Great. I'll be looking for them," said the woman as she walked down the street.

In the next few minutes, several other people stopped to admire the sculptures. A car even slowed down to look at them. "Too bad we can't talk to all these people," Stacey said. "It would be a great way to spread the word about the carnival."

Claudia's eyes brightened. "You just gave me an idea. Mrs. DeWitt said there were some art suplies we could use. Do you mind watching the kids for a minute? I'll be right back."

Stacey and the kids added some finishing touches to the dragon, draping Stacey's red scarf from its jaws for a tongue and attaching twig claws.

Soon Claudia returned with a piece of poster board and some markers. "I wanted to make a poster telling people about the carnival, but I knew I'd need help with the spelling, so I brought it out here."

With Stacey guiding her, Claudia made a bright, bold poster. "Come to the BSC Winter Carnival!" it read. Then it gave the date, time, and location.

The Barrett-DeWitt kids grabbed markers and started decorating the poster with drawings of snowflakes, snowmen, sleds, and steaming cups of hot chocolate.

"Excellent!" Claudia proclaimed, proudly propping the poster in front of the dragon.

"Wait — I have an idea," Stacey said, choosing a red marker. She picked up the poster and wrote something on it. When she was done, she set the poster back in place.

"Don't let winter drag-on," Lindsey gleefully read. "Come for fun." She turned her smiling, red-nosed face to Stacey and Claudia.

"That is so cute! I can't wait for the carnival."

"Neither can I," Claudia replied. It was true. She was really excited about the carnival. Kristy had come up with just the right idea to liven up the long, drawn-out winter.

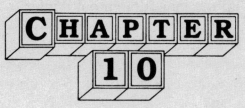

CHAPTER 10

Mom managed to obtain an appointment with Dr. Sherman, the specialist, for that Friday. Kristy had been very understanding when I said I had to miss another meeting.

I made a detour on the way home from school that Friday afternoon and took a bus downtown to Gloriana's House of Hair. I'd heard some horror stories about the place. (They'd totally annihilated Kristy's little stepsister's hair once.) But kids told me if I made an appointment with a stylist named Alexis, I'd be in good hands.

I settled into the chair and handed Alexis a picture of Anna. "That's what I want," I told her.

"No problem," Alexis replied, handing the photo back to me. "You want the same hairdo you had before you let it grow." Obviously Alexis thought I'd shown her a photo of myself with short hair. I simply nodded, not bothering to explain.

In half an hour, my hair looked just like Anna's.

"What do you think?" I asked as I burst through the front door.

Anna looked up at me. Her face was splotchy, her eyes red-rimmed. She'd been crying.

I went to the couch and sat beside her.

"I'm scared," Anna said, her voice a choked whisper. "I've been reading about scoliosis. What if I need surgery?"

"Dr. Abrams recommended the brace," I reminded her, putting my arm around her shoulders.

"But what if the brace hurts?" she asked, taking off her glasses and wiping her eyes. "What if it hurts so much I can't sit long enough to play the violin?"

"It won't," I assured her. "After all, Dr. Adams said it might make you *more* comfortable."

"I don't know," Anna said, getting off the couch. "Why did this have to happen to me?"

I felt bad for Anna. I didn't know how to make her feel better. I knew it was no time for one of my lame jokes. All I could say was what was in my heart. "I'll help you, Anna. Really, I will."

Turning toward me, she blinked hard. "Why did you cut your hair?"

"Because we're twins! It's a show of support, you know, like when a whole basketball team shaves their heads," I explained.

Anna nodded and smiled halfheartedly. "Thanks. I appreciate that a lot."

I cleared my throat. Suddenly my contacts were in danger of floating away. I blinked away the tears and checked my watch. "We'd better head out," I said.

"I know," Anna agreed glumly, going to the front hall closet for her jacket. As she zipped up she looked at me with the tiniest grin. "Your hair looks nice."

"Which one?" I joked.

Anna winced. "Seriously. It does look nice."

I smiled. "Sure it does. It looks like yours."

We took the train from the Stoneybrook station (just four minutes from our house, with Charlie driving) to Grand Central Station in Manhattan. Mom was waiting for us by the information booth. As soon as we met, she hurried us out to the street, where we hopped into a cab and rode uptown to Dr. Sherman's office.

I read magazines in the waiting room for what seemed like a million years while Anna and Mom were inside with the doctor. Finally, Dr. Sherman, a thin woman with frosted, permed hair and thick glasses, came out and asked me to join them.

"I think it would be nice for Anna if you stay with her while we make the mold for her brace," she said when I was in her office.

Mom was there, holding Anna's hand. Anna wasn't crying, but she looked pretty shaky.

"You're making it right now?" I asked, surprised that events were moving so quickly.

"Might as well," Dr. Sherman said. "The two orthopedic residents who assist me are here today, and they will do it. It can take up to two weeks to make the actual brace once we have the mold, so there's no sense delaying if we don't have to."

"How long will I have to wear it?" Anna asked in a small voice.

"Two years, maybe three. Twenty-three hours a day," Dr. Sherman said, propping herself on the edge of her desk. "A lot of it will depend on you. If you wear your brace all the time and do the exercises I give you, it will go faster than if you don't. We'll X ray you every three months to see how your curve is doing. If it seems to be getting better, then eventually you can start wearing the brace part-time."

"The low profile brace isn't a delight," she admitted frankly, "but you'll get used to it quickly, Anna. If you have the right attitude, it won't hold you back in any way."

"Will it hurt?" Anna asked.

"No," Dr. Sherman replied. "It may make you more comfortable. It will feel different, especially at first. If it chafes you can wear a soft undershirt between it and your skin. There won't be any pain though."

"Will I be able to play the violin?"

"Absolutely," Dr. Sherman assured her. "There's no reason why you can't."

A young man with a strawberry blond ponytail stuck his head in the door. "Are you ready for us?" he asked cheerfully.

"Ready," Dr. Sherman said. She nodded for us to follow her out of the room and down the hall to another room.

"I'm Dr. James," the young resident said, when Dr. Sherman left. He handed Anna a blue cotton robe and two items that looked like two giant pairs of pantyhose. "Those are body stockings," he explained. "Put them on, then put the robe over them to keep you warm. You can use the dressing room there."

"Why does she need two?" I asked.

"The plaster will adhere to one and the other will protect her skin," Dr. James explained.

Anna took the things from him and disappeared into the closet-size space. In minutes, she returned dressed in the body stockings and robe.

Dr. James explained what was going to happen next. "You'll take off the robe and we'll start putting strips of wet plaster on your torso," he said.

"Hey, Anna, you'll look just like one of Claudia's art projects," I joked.

"Lucky me," Anna replied with a wry smile.

"It's a little cold and gooey, but it doesn't hurt," Dr. James assured her. "The worst problem you'll have, Anna, is that you may feel tired from being still so long. We'll work as fast as we can, but we really need you to hold still."

"Okay, I'll do my best."

"Great," Dr. James said.

The second resident came in carrying a large tub of wet plaster. She was an African-American woman with short, black hair and a pretty face. "Hi, I'm Dr. Mays," she announced pleasantly. "We can get started now."

Anna had to take off her robe and stay there in just the body stockings, holding onto a bar that was anchored to the wall, something like a ballet *barre*. The body stockings were sheer, and I could tell that Anna felt embarrassed, but Dr. James and Dr. Mays talked to her constantly as they worked, joking about people on TV, rock stars, and so forth.

Mom and I sat on stools watching. Mom looked serious, but she broke into a quick smile from time to time.

I tried to be lighthearted and joined in with the residents. Taking a banana from my backpack, I held it up as if it were a microphone. "And now for a special report on multicultural traditions," I said, imitating a reporter. "I'm here interviewing Anna Stevenson, the world's first human piñata." Anna mostly rolled her eyes at my jokes, but at least it was taking her mind off things.

"You guys look so much alike," Dr. Mays commented as she knelt beside Anna, smoothing a plaster strip around her waist.

"Thanks," I said.

"No, we don't," Anna said, our voices overlapping.

Our eyes met in an awkward gaze. I felt hurt that Anna had denied we look alike. The expression on her face told me she wished she'd kept her mouth shut.

"Well, I guess we look more alike now that Abby cut her hair," Anna said quickly. Then she sighed. "But once I start wearing this brace we'll look different again."

"Not that different," Dr. James said as he dipped a long gauze strip into the tub of plaster. "You'll just look slightly heavier because of the brace. But you're so slim now it's nothing to worry about."

"Will she need larger clothing?" Mom asked.

"Probably one size larger, that's all," Dr. Mays replied. "Also, some girls who wear braces are more comfortable in pants that stretch at the waist."

"You'll want to start wearing T-shirts or undershirts between you and the brace," Dr. James added. "It will give you some padding, especially in the beginning, when you're adjusting to the feel of it."

"They make great undershirts and camisoles nowadays," Mom commented.

"They sure do," Dr. Mays agreed. "Besides, this winter's been so cold, I wear a thermal undershirt over my bra just for the warmth."

While Mom and Dr. Mays discussed the wonders of thermal underwear, my mind raced. All this discussion about new clothing had given me a great idea. I knew the perfect way to cheer up Anna.

I decided to set my plan in motion the moment we arrived home. It was a brilliant idea, and Anna was going to adore it!

CHAPTER 11

The first person I called for help was Stacey. She has awesome fashion sense.

"Mom gave me two hundred dollars to spend," I told Stacey over the phone the next day, Saturday. "I'm going to buy Anna an entire new wardrobe."

"Not for two hundred dollars you're not," Stacey disagreed. "But you can probably find her several nice new things, enough to start her off."

Two hundred dollars had seemed like a fortune when I approached Mom with my idea last night and she offered me the money.

I saw Stacey's point, though. Clothing is expensive, and even inexpensive clothing isn't cheap.

"If I'm careful I should be able to buy about ten things, don't you think?" I asked hopefully.

"Seven or eight," Stacey speculated more cautiously. Since Stacey is not only a fashion pro but a math whiz, I took her word for it. Seven or eight new items would be good enough. I could just imagine Anna's happy face when I presented the new clothing to her. It would be all bright, new, and ready to wear over her brace. It had to cheer her up.

"So, will you come with me?" I asked Stacey.

"Sure. You know me. I love to shop for clothes."

"Great. My mother will drive us to the mall. We'll pick you up in a half hour," I said before hanging up. With my hand still resting on the phone, I sat for a moment in the quiet kitchen. Anna and Mom were still asleep, which was unusual for them. But we'd arrived home late the night before.

Yesterday, the mold had taken a while to dry. Sitting and sitting, just waiting, was hard for Anna. (It would have driven me completely out of my mind.) I tried to make the time go faster by sitting beside her and discussing the different sports stars featured in the office copies of *Sports Illustrated*. She didn't seem all that interested, so I found a crossword puzzle in another magazine. We did that together for awhile.

When they finally sawed through the plaster cast, the mold looked really neat — an exact model of Anna's body, every curve and bend of it.

I was about to go upstairs and wake Mom when she appeared in the kitchen, already dressed. "Ready to go?" she asked, yawning.

We left a note for Anna and climbed into the car. After picking up Stacey, Mom dropped us off at the mall.

"We could try Laura Ashley," Stacey suggested, gazing at the clothing store in front of us. "I think the clothes in there would fit Anna's style."

I gazed at the mannequin in the front window. She was dressed in a floral print corduroy jumper over a ruffled blouse. "It looks kind of young, don't you think?" I asked.

"I've seen Anna wear Laura Ashley dresses before," Stacey insisted.

"Maybe. But the residents who made her brace suggested stretchy stuff. They said that would be the most comfortable over the brace."

"We could go to Macy's or Lear's," Stacey suggested.

"All right," I agreed. "Lear's is closest. Let's start there."

After about an hour of shopping, I wondered if I'd overestimated Stacey's fashion sense. I didn't know what was wrong with her that morning. She kept selecting outfits that were kind of basic and plain. It wasn't the way *she* dressed. I couldn't tell what she was thinking.

"I'm trying to picture Anna and pick outfits I can imagine her wearing," Stacey explained after I'd rejected yet another of her choices, a simple black pull-on skirt.

Obviously, she wasn't picturing Anna very well. "Look at me," I suggested. "I look just like her. Use me as your guide."

"But you're not like Anna," Stacey protested, draping the skirt over her arm.

"Not like her? We're twins! How much more alike can we be?"

"But your personalities aren't alike," Stacey insisted.

"I know, but what looks good on me would look good on her, right? We're the same."

Stacey sighed and hung the skirt back on the rack. "If you say so."

"Besides, I don't want to buy her drab, everyday stuff. I want to give Anna bright, fun things, clothes that will cheer her up. Come on," I said, pulling Stacey by the arm. "The problem is we're not in the right department."

"But we're in Juniors."

"No. *This* is the right department," I insisted, pointing to the sign ahead of us that read Junior Sportswear.

"Abby," Stacey began, "are you sure?"

"Absolutely. The clothing here is stretchy and comfortable. And if she has the right clothes Anna will want to do her excercises."

It didn't take long for me to spend that two hundred dollars. Stacey had been right about that.

I was pleased with my choices, though. I bought Anna a silky jogging outfit in a bright pattern of blue and pink; a pair of shiny yellow bike pants; two big sweatshirts, one orange and one yellow (I figured she could wear them with the bike pants); a fuzzy purple sweatsuit; and a baseball cap. All the material was soft, and all the clothes were either stretchy or loose-fitting. I double-checked everything to make sure I'd chosen the right sizes. The colors were bright, so Anna would feel cheerful when she looked at herself. All in all, I thought I'd zeroed in on the perfect things.

I paid for everything, and the bill came to two hundred and twelve dollars and twenty cents. Luckily, I had some of my baby-sitting money with me to pay for the extra. I didn't mind spending it. The expression on Anna's face would be well worth the money.

I called Mom from a pay phone in Lear's lobby and she left to pick us up. We window-shopped for a half hour, then went to meet her.

"Can you believe it hasn't snowed in four

whole days, counting today?" Stacey commented on the way home, as she gazed out the car window.

"Thank goodness," Mom said, turning onto Elm Street, where Stacey lives.

Stacey laughed. "My mom feels the same way. She's sick of shoveling and worrying about getting to work on time. But *I'm* getting worried about our winter carnival plans. What if it doesn't snow between now and then?"

"Not snow in the next two weeks?" I scoffed. "The way this winter has been going? Not likely!"

We pulled into Stacey's driveway. "I suppose you're right," she said.

"Thank you for your help," I called as she climbed out of the car.

"I didn't do anything," she said with a laugh. "You picked it all out."

"True," I admitted. "But thanks for coming."

"You're welcome. I hope Anna likes it all."

"She will."

"So you found some things Anna will like?" Mom said on the way home.

"Definitely. Should we give them to her now, or wait until she has the brace?"

"I don't know. She did seem a bit down last night. Maybe she could use something to cheer her up right now."

"Okay!" I was excited about the clothes and would have found it hard to wait.

When we arrived home, Anna was sitting at the kitchen table paging through a music magazine. "Hi," she said, shifting her eyes up from the article she was reading. "Where'd you guys go?"

"Didn't you see my note?" Mom asked, looking at the note on the counter.

Anna glanced at it. "Oh, I didn't notice."

"We were at the mall," I said, placing my shopping bags on top of her magazine. I was bursting with excitement. "Wait until you see what I bought for you!"

"For me?" Anna asked.

"Yes! Check it out!"

Anna reached in and pulled the jogging suit out first. She looked a little bewildered. "This one isn't for me, is it?"

"Yeah," I said.

"But I don't jog."

"You don't have to jog," I explained, pulling up a kitchen chair beside her. "It's just something comfortable and pretty to wear."

Anna checked the tag. "But this isn't my size."

Mom and I glanced at one another uncomfortably.

"Oh, I forgot," said Anna. "It will be."

"That doesn't matter," I said encouragingly.

96

"Look at these!" I dug into the bag and found the yellow bike pants. "Aren't they awesome? I bought shirts to match, too." I laid them out on the table. "And here's the finishing touch." I took out the baseball hat and plunked it on her head. "You are going to look so outrageous that no one will even notice you're a little bulkier."

Anna took off the cap and turned it in her hands. She looked down at it, then up at me. "Thanks, Abby. You've gone to a lot of trouble and I appreciate it a lot."

Despite her words she didn't look very enthusiastic about the new clothing.

If great new clothes didn't cheer her up, then she was more depressed than I'd imagined.

I was going to have to work even harder in the next few weeks to keep up her spirits.

CHAPTER 12

The next week seemed to drag on forever. Cheering someone up can be incredibly hard work. Anna didn't complain a lot; she was just very quiet.

The only thing she seemed to enjoy was playing her violin. And even that she did with a quiet intensity, as if she were simply glad to forget about everything and lose herself in the music. She may have been enjoying herself in her own way, but it didn't look as if she were exactly having *fun*.

I was determined to help her.

Believe me, I tried.

"The BSC winter carnival is coming up," I reminded her one gray Saturday morning. "Remember, you're working with Mary Anne in the hot chocolate booth."

"What are you talking about?" she asked, looking up from the book she was reading.

"Don't you remember? I told you, I volunteered you to work on the carnival."

"You did? Why?"

"Because you need something to do, to take your mind off the brace."

"No, I don't."

"Yes, you do. You haven't done anything but hang around the house and read and watch TV and play the violin. You're just brooding."

"I'm not brooding. I'm coming to terms with it, that's all. Besides, it's winter, Abby. It's cold and miserable outside. What do you want me to do?"

"Something fun! Like work on the winter carnival with me. It'll be a blast."

Anna smiled, although she looked like she didn't want to. "You're too much," she said. "You're impossible to say no to."

"That's because you know I'm right."

Anna glanced out the window. "You're not going to have much of a winter carnival if it doesn't snow soon."

"It'll snow," I said confidently.

On the following Saturday, Anna and Mom were scheduled to go to the city to pick up the brace. "When's our train?" I asked.

"Mom and I are going on the ten o'clock express," Anna answered.

"What do you mean, 'Mom and I'? I'm going, too."

Anna chewed on her lower lip and picked at a thread on her sweater. "Would you mind not coming?"

"Not coming?" Had I heard her right? "Why not?"

"I don't know," she replied, looking up at me. "I just want this to be over with, and somehow it seems like . . . like a much bigger deal when you're around."

I didn't understand this at all.

"It has nothing to do with you," Anna added quickly. "It's me. Okay? I just need to do this my way."

"Sure. No problem."

After Anna and Mom left, I stood in the quiet house and a feeling of loneliness washed over me. It was horrible. I *was* hurt. I wanted to help Anna. So I called Kristy and, as I'd hoped she would, she invited me to her house. She and I spent the afternoon placing winter carnival fliers around our neighborhood.

Mom and Anna were gone all day. It turned out that the brace had to be carefully fitted, with a million little adjustments that could only be made once Anna tried it on.

By the time they returned home, they looked tired, especially Anna. "Let's see it," I said.

Anna lifted up her shirt and I could see the molded plastic brace, which she was wearing over a thin sleeveless T-shirt. I nodded, not knowing what to say. We'd looked at plenty of pictures, but actually seeing it, up close and personal, was different. I swallowed hard.

"It's not as bad as it looks," Anna said.

"Can I try it on?" I asked, wanting to share this experience with Anna, to know what she would be going through. To make it easier for her, if I could.

"I'd rather you didn't," Anna said.

"Why not?"

"It won't fit you, Abby. It was made for me."

I touched the brace. "It has to be pretty close," I insisted.

"Stop it, already!" Anna snapped.

Stunned, I pulled away my hand. "All right!"

With tears brimming in her eyes, Anna stormed upstairs.

Feeling bewildered, I turned to Mom. "I didn't mean to upset her. What'd I do wrong?"

Mom shook her head wearily. "She's tired. It's been a very trying day. Give her some space for awhile."

Space? I didn't think so. She needed my help. I would have to redouble my efforts.

On Sunday, Anna wore her brace around the house under her big flannel nightgown. "How does it feel?" I asked.

"It doesn't hurt at all. It's a little weird, though," she replied, moving stiffly from the kitchen table to the living room couch.

"What's weird about it?" I pressed. The more I knew, the more I could help.

"I can't really bend at the waist the way I'm used to," she answered, "and it's rubbing against my right hip bone."

"Are you wearing a shirt under it?"

Anna nodded. "But the material is bunching around my hip. Maybe I should try one of the lighter undershirts Mom bought me."

"I feel awful for you," I said sympathetically. "It must be so confining. So restricting. I'd hate it."

"It's really a lot less restricting than I expected. I think once I get used to moving a little differently — you know, stooping to get things instead of bending, for instance — it will be all right. Dr. Sherman said I'll get used to it soon enough."

"You're so brave," I commented, full of admiration.

On Monday, it still hadn't snowed. I was glad of that, though. It meant Anna wouldn't have to maneuver through snow and ice on her first day going to school with the brace. She came downstairs wearing a sweater and black stretch leggings over her brace. The outfit looked all right, but it bulged a little, in places, now that she had the brace underneath. "Why don't you wear one of the outfits I bought you?" I suggested.

"Um . . . uh . . ." Anna stammered. "I'm saving them . . . for the nicer weather."

"Oh, I suppose that makes sense," I said as I held Anna's jacket up to help her get into it.

She took the jacket from me and put it on herself. "Ready," she said, leaning over stiffly to lift her backpack from the couch.

"Here, take my arm," I offered, raising my arm to her as we walked out of the house.

"I don't need your arm," she said firmly. "There's nothing wrong with my legs."

"Excuse me. I thought you might be off balance," I replied coldly.

"Sorry," she muttered.

I tried to stick close to Anna that day in case she needed help. It was hard, though, because our schedules are very different.

All through the school day, I worried about Anna. What if she dropped her books and couldn't bend down to pick them up? She'd be mortified if she had to ask for help. I know I would be.

What if someone made a comment or teased her? Anna would probably take the insult and suffer in silence.

She really needed me, and it was killing me not to be there for her. By the time I saw Anna again after school, I was dying to hear how her day had gone.

I spotted her coming down the hall toward

my locker. Before she reached me, Alan Gray came barreling into the hall from a classroom. Not looking where he was going at all, he smashed right into Anna.

"Oh, no!" I cried, rushing toward her as Anna bounced into the lockers, flailed her arms for balance, and slid down to the floor, her books scattering everywhere.

"I'm okay, I'm okay," said Anna.

"Whoa!" Alan gasped, reaching out to help pull Anna up. "Sorry. I didn't see you. I'm glad that didn't hurt you. But, man, that hurt me. You must have hard bones. Either that or you're wearing metal underwear."

Metal underwear! The words rang in my head like an alarm. How could he say such a thing?

"Take your hands off her!" I shouted, ripping Alan's hand out of Anna's.

"It was just an accident," Alan protested.

"Just get away from my sister!" I told him angrily.

"Abby!" Anna gasped. "Stop it!"

"You watch your fat mouth, Alan Gray!" I cried.

"You're nuts, Abby," Alan said, backing away. "Completely gone."

"That's what I want you to be!" I shouted at him. "Completely gone."

When I turned back to Anna, tears were rolling down her cheeks. "Are you hurt?" I asked.

She shook her head, still crying. "It's your feelings that are hurt, I know," I said. "What a jerk he is! He's so — "

"It's not him. It's you!" Anna cried angrily, wiping her eyes.

"Me?!"

"Yes, it's you. You're driving me crazy!"

"Listen, Anna, I know Alan upset you but — "

"Alan didn't upset me!" she yelled. "It was an accident, Abby. He didn't mean to do it."

"I know, but he said . . ."

"He didn't know what he was saying. He doesn't know I'm wearing a brace. He was making a joke. A *joke*."

I folded my arms defensively. "Well, it wasn't funny."

"It would have been all right if you hadn't gone crazy. You humiliated me."

"I didn't. He did!" I shouted.

"No, *you* did."

This was unbelievable. I breathed deeply, trying to remember that Anna probably had had a very hard day. She wasn't herself.

"Come on," I said, taking her arm. "We're going down to the Civic Center pool. You need to swim."

Anna yanked her arm away. "I'm not swimming. Forget it."

"You have to swim," I said. "We've both read the literature Mom brought home, and I'm sure you remember what Dr. Abrams said. Exercise will keep your muscles strong, which helps support your spine."

"I don't feel like exercising, all right?"

"No, not all right!" Somewhere, in a corner of my mind, I was aware that I was shouting, but I couldn't stop. "If you don't exercise, your curve won't improve."

"*We* don't have scoliosis," Anna shot back. "I do."

"Did I say 'we'?"

"Yes, and that's exactly how you've been acting, like this is your problem. This is *my* back, Abby, *my* problem, and I'm dealing with it in my own way. This isn't about you — believe it or not."

"I know it's your back. I've been thinking about you from the start and trying to help."

"But it isn't helping. You've been acting like this is happening to you. You keep trying to make me do things you want to do. You volunteered me to work on the carnival. You even bought me clothes only you would wear."

"You don't like the clothes?" I asked, stunned.

"No! When have you ever seen me wear

106

clothes like that? I'm your twin, Abby, and you act like you don't even know who I am."

"Maybe I *don't* know," I repeated hollowly. "I never thought you could be so ungrateful and self-centered."

Stung by my words, Anna turned her back to me. Then, very carefully, she squatted down and began picking up her books.

Angry as I was, I knelt down to help her.

Glaring at me, she snatched away the book I had picked up.

"Fine, be that way!" I exclaimed. "Do everything for yourself. See if I care."

Anna didn't reply but continued furiously gathering her books.

"What?" I said, standing up. "You're not talking to me now?"

Anna just glowered at me.

"That's okay with me," I told her. "It'll be a relief not to talk to you." Then I stormed to my locker without looking back.

CHAPTER 13

Anna and I didn't speak to one another for the rest of the week. At first it was easy, because I was so furious with her. I had no desire to speak to her. After all the effort and care I'd put into helping her, she'd told me I was no help. It hurt my feelings. It wasn't fair or right.

Maybe I *had* gone a little crazy with Alan Gray, but I'd spent the entire day worrying about Anna. In my mind, all my fears were coming true when he said that metal underwear thing.

She could have shown a little understanding about that, just as I was trying to understand her dark moods. I was angry at her, but mostly I felt hurt. Anna acted as though I were some kind of spoiled brat who was annoyed because I wasn't the center of attention. She was so wrong.

By Wednesday the feud was wearing me down. It was depressing. "What's wrong?" Mary Anne asked at our meeting.

"It's Anna," I replied. Before I knew it, I was pouring out the story to my BSC friends.

"I knew she wouldn't like those clothes," Stacey said.

"Why didn't you say something, then?" I asked.

"I tried, but you seemed so sure of what you wanted for her."

Was that what had happened? Possibly. I come on too strong sometimes. I know that, but I'm not always aware when I'm doing it. Had I done it with Anna, too?

"She'll realize you were only trying to help," Mary Anne said. "You'll see."

"This is a really hard time for her," Kristy added.

"It sounds like it's been kind of a hard time for you too," Jessi added.

"It has," I admitted. "But why should it be? Nothing's happened to me."

"Maybe it's because you're twins," Mary Anne suggested. "You must feel so helpless seeing your twin going through something you can't do anything about."

I appreciated Mary Anne's understanding more than I can say.

"Why don't you go home and try to make up?" Mary Anne suggested.

I shook my head. "I can't."

"Why not?"

"I don't know. I just can't."

Why couldn't I? I suppose I was still angry with Anna. My pride was hurt too. She'd made me feel like an idiot. Part of me desperately wanted to set things right, but I knew I wasn't ready to bring myself to try. Maybe I was simply afraid to hear more harsh words from Anna.

When I returned home that night, Anna left the living room the moment I entered it. "What's going on?" Mom asked as she watched Anna dash up the stairs.

I told her everything. "Oh, dear." She sighed. "I was afraid this was coming."

"You were?"

She nodded. "Abby, let me ask you something. Do you feel guilty that this has happened to Anna and not to you?"

"Why should I feel guilty? I can't do anything about it."

"I know, that's logical," Mom said, drawing me down next to her on the couch. "But how do you *feel*?"

Unexpectedly, tears rushed into my eyes. "Lonely," I said. "Afraid."

"What are you afraid of?" Mom asked gently.

"That Anna and I won't be twins anymore," I cried. "I know that's silly but . . ."

Mom hugged me. "It's not silly."

"Why does she have to wear a brace and not me?" I sobbed into her shoulder.

Mom smoothed my hair. "I don't know, honey, but it's not your fault."

I nodded and wiped my eyes. "Then why do I feel that it *is* my fault? Why do I feel this is all so wrong?"

"Because you believe in fairness, Abby, and some things simply aren't fair."

On Thursday, I actually made the effort to say hello to Anna at breakfast, but she looked away. Stung — and a little angered by her rejection — I didn't try again.

"How are things with Anna and you?" Mary Anne asked at our Friday meeting.

"Terrible," I replied.

"There's more good news," Kristy said. "I hate to say this, but I'm afraid we're going to have to cancel the winter carnival."

"No way!" Claudia cried.

"Why?" asked Mallory.

Kristy gestured toward the window. "No snow. I could see the mud and grass on my lawn this morning."

"But it's still winter," Stacey argued. "We don't need snow for it to be winter."

"Stacey, think about what we have planned," Kristy said, sitting forward in her chair. "A snow sculpture contest, sled races, snow painting, a snowball throwing booth, a snowshoe walking competition."

"Okay, okay," Stacey said glumly. "We do need snow for all of that."

"Even hot chocolate is a lot less appealing when it's nearly forty degrees," Jessi added.

"Can't we try, though? I mean, how are we going to tell people?" Claudia wondered.

"Maybe I could call the radio station," Kristy said. "They're always announcing cancellations. And then we can all just go over to Mary Anne's and turn away anyone who doesn't hear about it over the radio. That's the only way I can think of handling the situation."

One person I wouldn't have to tell about it was Anna. Although I'd volunteered her to work on the carnival, it was obvious she wanted nothing to do with it.

Just then, the phone rang. As Claudia talked to the client, I wondered how long my fight with Anna would last. Surely it couldn't last forever.

Surely I wouldn't have to say to people: "That was the year Anna and I stopped being twins."

The very idea made me shudder. I felt terrible. No snow. No winter carnival. And worst of all, no Anna.

How had things become so hopeless?

CHAPTER 14

saturday

weather is weird. Just when
you think you know what it's
going to do, it takes you by
surprise. There must be a
comparison to life buried
somewhere in that statement.
I don't know. All I do know
is that this time the weather
really sent us scrambling.

Stacey had to tell me what happened Saturday morning because I was home with an asthma attack. It was a mild one — my over-the-counter inhaler did the trick — but Mom didn't want me going out right after it. Besides, I saw no reason to. The carnival was probably canceled. It wasn't crucial that I be at Mary Anne's to help tell people to go home. My friends could handle that without me, I was sure.

At least that's what I thought.

Everyone else thought so, too. The morning was as bleak and snow-free as the days preceding it had been.

Kristy had called Stacey that morning to report that she hadn't been able to persuade the radio station to make her announcement. "It doesn't fit into their format, they told me," Kristy said, sounding disgusted.

Stacey rolled her eyes. "Too bad we didn't put posters all over town. Then we could run around and write 'canceled' on them."

"True. Oh, well. Can you meet at Mary Anne's and be part of the turn-away committee?"

"Sure," Stacey agreed. "I'll have to bring Charlotte Johanssen with me, though. I'm sitting for her this morning. Is that all right?"

"No problem," Kristy replied. "I'll have

Karen and Andrew with me. Jessi's bringing Becca along. Mallory has to watch her brothers and sisters, and Claudia is helping her. Mary Anne's minding the Hill kids. Definitely bring Char along. Having the kids there will make everything less depressing."

Stacey walked to Charlotte's, and Dr. Johanssen dropped the girls at Mary Anne's old farmhouse on Burnt Hill Road. When they arrived, everyone was milling around by the barn. Claudia and Mallory were kneeling just inside the open barn door, working on a sign to tell people the carnival wasn't going to happen.

"Hey, what was that?" Charlotte asked as she and Stacey walked toward the others.

"What was what?" Stacey asked.

"Something wet landed on my nose."

Then Stacey felt it, too. Gazing up, she noticed tiny, almost invisible bits of snow blowing in the air.

"Hey! Snow!" Nicky Pike shouted.

Everyone turned their faces upward to see it. The flakes were so light, so . . . invisible, almost . . . that no one dared to feel too excited. Still . . .

Claudia and Mallory stopped making their sign. "What do you think?" Claud asked Kristy.

"It'll probably stop soon," Kristy replied cautiously.

In minutes, though, the flakes grew thicker and began falling faster. "I think this is real snow," Mary Anne said hopefully.

Stacey stepped into the barn doorway for cover and watched as everything around her became dusted in whiteness.

The kids were the first to become excited. "Snow! Snow! Snow!" Margo Pike sang out as she spread her arms wide and twirled amid the falling flakes.

"It's snowing! It's snowing!" cried Sara Hill, bouncing as if she had invisible springs on her feet.

Soon all the kids were dancing and jumping, sticking out their tongues to catch falling flakes, examining individual snowflakes, which were rapidly attaching themselves to their gloves and scarves.

Stacey looked to Kristy and caught her eye. "It's sticking," Stacey said.

"You're right," Kristy agreed.

Claudia smiled broadly. "Let's do it," she suggested. "Let's go ahead with the carnival."

"Can we?" Mary Anne asked. "Is there enough time?"

"Sure there is!" Kristy declared, clapping her gloves together. "But we will really have to move."

Kristy is always at her best when something has to be done, and as Stacey told me later, this time she was totally awesome. She assigned everyone to groups, including the kids. Mallory and Claudia mobilized the Pike crew to bring tables out of the barn and set them up, as we had originally planned. Sara and Norman Hill, along with Karen and Andrew Brewer, joined Kristy in putting up the signs we'd painted, showing which booths were which. Mary Anne, Jessi, and Stacey took Charlotte and Becca inside to start the hot chocolate and to unwrap the baked brownies and cookies, which had been prepared ahead of time.

As they scurried around in the falling snow, everyone seemed to be in a great mood. Mary Anne's dad saw what was happening, and even he caught the spirit. He hooked up the stereo speakers so that they faced out into the yard, then he put on tapes. The first song he played was "Winter Wonderland."

"This *is* a winter wonderland!" Charlotte exclaimed, hugging Stacey.

"It sure is," Stacey agreed. "What good luck!"

It must have been around that time that she called me from Mary Anne's kitchen phone. "Come over right now if you're feeling better," she said. "We're having so much fun."

As I listened, I glanced out the window at the swirling snow. Everything looked as if it were inside one of those glass snow globes.

"You know what?" Stacey continued. "See if Shannon can come over with you. And bring Anna, too. She'll love it."

I was feeling much better, and Stacey's excitement was catching. It made me eager to be part of things. "I'll be there as soon as I can," I assured her.

I called Shannon right away. "I already told Kristy that I can't make it over there until this afternoon," she said. "I can work a booth when I get there." She paused, then added, "I bet Maria and Tiffany would help."

"All right. I'll tell everyone," I agreed.

When I hung up, I noticed that Anna was in the kitchen doorway watching me. Her expression told me she was interested, but when I faced her she turned away.

"I'm going to the winter carnival," I said to the back of her head. "I don't suppose you'd be interested in coming along."

Without turning, she walked silently out of the room.

I stuck my tongue out at the place where she'd been standing. "Be that way," I muttered. "See if I care."

That was the problem, though. I did care.

CHAPTER 15

By the time Mom dropped me off at Mary Anne's, Burnt Hill Road was lined with parked cars. People had flocked to the carnival. Why not? It was a fun thing to do on the first snowy day in two weeks.

I joined Stacey at our snow painting booth. For a nickel, kids could squirt paint on the snow, using the special colors we'd bought at the mall. They had three minutes to create their masterpieces. In a brilliant last-minute inspiration, Kristy had suggested that Mary Anne run inside for her Polaroid camera. For an additional dime, the kids could purchase a photo of their artwork.

I took the photos and gave Stacey a hand as she helped the kids with the spray bottles. Just keeping them filled had me hopping. The booth was a great success. Kids loved adding colors to the fresh, white snow. And the steady snowfall meant that soon after each picture was finished and photographed, it was covered with more snow, so there was a brand new space for the next artist to use. "This couldn't have worked out better," Stacey remarked.

After awhile, I took a break and wandered over to Mary Anne and Jessi who were doing a brisk business selling treats. The brownies were already gone. "My parents are having a great time," Mary Anne reported. "Richard's flipping tapes and Sharon's inside baking us some more brownies."

"Excellent," I replied, as Jessi poured me a cup of mint-flavored hot chocolate from a thermos. "This stuff was worth the extra money," I commented after tasting it.

"It's the best," Jessi agreed.

I gazed around at the carnival. I noticed Mr. Ramsey walking around with Squirt on his shoulders. Squirt's tongue was out as he tried to catch snowflakes on it. Beside them, Mrs. Ramsey and Jessi's aunt Cecelia admired the shiny silver paper snowflake Becca had cut out at the snowflake booth. Beside the barn, Norman Hill helped his mother steady one of the plastic sleds as she prepared to make a downhill run with Sara. Byron and Adam Pike collected quarters from the people who were lined up for a chance to go down the hill.

Closer to the house, Claudia was running

around like crazy, organizing the people who wanted to compete in the snow sculpture contest. Mallory was dipping into a big cardboard box we'd assembled several days earlier. It was filled with props and costumes of every kind. Mallory was handing out at a steady rate hats, scarves, plastic pipes, yarn wigs, and every imaginable item. As I watched, she passed a boy a fake hand left over from Halloween. (I could just imagine that kid's sculpture.)

Dropping my empty cup into a garbage can (thoughtfully provided by the BSC, of course), I was about to return to help Stacey when I noticed Shannon coming into the yard with Maria and Tiffany.

Anna was with them.

My first impulse was to join them, but then I remembered Anna and I were fighting and I turned away. Why had she come here, anyway? Certainly not because I invited her. Was it for the chance to ignore me in public?

When I turned back, I saw that Shannon had joined Kristy in organizing the next snowshoe race. (Kristy had found some old tennis rackets in her attic and rigged them so they could be attached to kids' boots with Velcro straps.)

Maria and Tiffany were helping at the refreshment stand.

Where was Anna? My eyes searched the

crowd. When I spotted her, my jaw dropped in shock.

Anna was on the short sled-ride line, waiting her turn.

What was she doing?

Without thinking, I charged over to her and grabbed her arm. "Do you have your brace on?" I hissed.

Anna turned away.

"Anna! Do you have your brace on?"

"Yes," she answered me angrily through gritted teeth.

"Good. But you can't go on that ride. You'll hurt yourself."

"No, I won't." She patted her waist. "I have added protection on."

"Anna, don't be — " I didn't have time to finish, because Anna's turn had come. She took the plastic sled from Adam Pike.

She couldn't possibly steer that thing. How could she, when she couldn't bend? She'd crash, or tip over, or fly off. Then she'd be hurt — and humiliated. I couldn't let her do it.

I was just about to rush to her and pull the sled from her hands when a picture flashed into my mind. It was an image of the scene I'd made in school when I'd lashed out at a poor, clueless Alan Gray.

Stop and cool down, I commanded myself. It took every ounce of energy I had.

And, in the moment it took me to stop and say this to myself, Anna took off on the sled, laughing as she zoomed down the hill.

"Anna!" I screamed, racing to the bottom of the sled course.

I reached her as the sled slowed at the foot of the hill. My heart raced as I watched it slow and finally stop.

Anna gazed up at me. Her face was bright, her eyes sparkling. "See? I'm fine." She reached out her hand, and I helped pull her to her feet. "I'm fine," she repeated.

Looking at her smiling, proud face I realized something. She *was* fine. But she'd needed to know that. And now she did know it. And she'd showed me, too.

All the fussing I'd done around her, all the worrying, the picking things up for her, the overprotecting — all that had made her feel as though her normal life had ended. It had made her feel she wasn't fine.

I'd made her feel worse, not better.

"I'm sorry," I said.

"I'm sorry too," Anna replied.

"What for?" I asked, surprised.

"Because you've been trying to help me and I've been pushing you away. This has been hard for me, and I guess I just needed to make my own way through it, without you . . . I don't know . . ."

"Without me making you feel like you were helpless," I suggested.

Anna laughed. "Yeah, that's it. But you were being so nice and I was so cold."

"That's all right," I said honestly. "I'd have driven me crazy too. I know I go overboard. I thought I was trying to help, but I know part of it was that I was just trying to keep us together — for my own sake."

"We'll always be twins," Anna said seriously. "And I'm glad of that. We have our differences, though. You have to try to remember that."

"It isn't fair that you have to go through this alone," I said.

"You go through asthma by yourself," Anna reminded me.

"That's different," I objected.

"How?"

I shrugged. "I don't know."

"It's not different," she insisted.

She was right, although I'd never thought of it that way. "I suppose," I conceded. "Okay, from now on I'll stop trying to do everything for you. I promise. Unless, of course, you ask."

"I do have one request," Anna said, draping her arm across my shoulder.

"Anything!" I replied as we headed toward the refreshment booth. "You name it."

"Could we go to the mall tomorrow and exchange those clothes you bought me?"

"You really hate them, huh?"

"They're the worst."

I laughed, then sighed. "Some people have no taste."

"And could you grow your hair back, please? That cut looks much better on me," Anna added, grining.

"I know what you mean. "You just don't have the face for wearing your hair long like me. I have the cheekbones to carry it off. You don't."

Anna punched me playfully in the arm. "We have the exact same cheekbones!" Then her face grew serious. "Listen, Abby," she said, "I'm going to do everything I have to do to make this work. I'm going to wear the brace as much as necessary. I'll do my exercises. You can do them with me if you like, but you don't have to. I'll do them with or without you. I'm not going to feel sorry for myself. We discovered the problem in time. Honestly, I'm okay about this."

At that moment, I knew the worst of the crisis was over. Sure, there might be rough times ahead. But they couldn't tear Anna and me apart. We weren't clones; we were twins, connected in a way that nothing could ever change. We'd always be together no matter what curves (spinal or otherwise) life threw at

126

us. And maybe that's what being twins is really all about.

I looked at the sled run, then at Anna. "Bet I could beat you down that hill," I said.

"Could not."

"Could so."

"Let's just see."

The line was short and we were soon sitting on sleds poised at the top of the hill. "Ready, set . . ." Anna began, her eyes sparkling.

"Go!" I finished, pushing off. Anna pushed off beside me. As we sped toward the bottom of the hill, I knew that no matter who got there first, we would both walk away feeling like winners.

Dear Reader,

I never had scoliosis, but it is a common condition. In fact, many people — both older and younger — suggested that I write a book about scoliosis. That's how *Abby's Twin* began.

You are probably familiar with the school screening that Abby and Anna had in this book. It's natural to be concerned about this testing, but as Abby and Anna learn, you don't have to be afraid of scoliosis. Though Abby overreacts to Anna's situation (as she does in many situations), she eventually comes to realize that Anna will still be able to do everything she used to do — especially play the violin!

If you have questions about scoliosis or would like to learn more about it, you can talk to your school nurse or family doctor. Hopefully, Anna and Abby have helped you understand scoliosis a little bit better.

Happy reading,

Ann M Martin

Ann M. Martin

About the Author

ANN MATTHEWS MARTIN was born on August 12, 1955. She grew up in Princeton, NJ, with her parents and her younger sister, Jane.

Although Ann used to be a teacher and then an editor of children's books, she's now a full-time writer. She gets the ideas for her books from many different places. Some are based on personal experiences. Others are based on childhood memories and feelings. Many are written about contemporary problems or events.

All of Ann's characters, even the members of the Baby-sitters Club, are made up. (So is Stoneybrook.) But many of her characters are based on real people. Sometimes Ann names her characters after people she knows, other times she chooses names she likes.

In addition to the Baby-sitters Club books, Ann Martin has written many other books for children. Her favorite is *Ten Kids, No Pets* because she loves big families and she loves animals. Her favorite Baby-sitters Club book is *Kristy's Big Day*. (By the way, Kristy is her favorite baby-sitter!)

Ann M. Martin now lives in New York with her cats, Gussie and Woody. Her hobbies are reading, sewing, and needlework — especially making clothes for children.

Notebook Pages

This Baby-sitters Club book belongs to _____.

I am _____ years old and in the _____

grade.

The name of my school is _____.

I got this BSC book from _____.

I started reading it on _____ and

finished reading it on _____.

The place where I read most of this book is _____.

My favorite part was when _____.

If I could change anything in the story, it might be the part when

_____.

My favorite character in the Baby-sitters Club is _____.

The BSC member I am most like is _____

because _____.

If I could write a Baby-sitters Club book it would be about _____

_____.

#104 Abby's Twin

Abby and Anna look the same, but have very different personalities. The person who could be my twin is _____
_____. Some of the similarities we share
are _____
_____
_____ Some of our differences are _____
_____
_____ When Anna is diag-
nosed with scoliosis, she faces a big challenge. The biggest
challenge I ever faced was when _____
_____
_____ Anna rises to her
challenge by wearing her brace, doing her excercises, and
listening to her doctors. This is how I dealt with my challenge:
_____
_____ At first, Abby
isn't a help to Anna (although she *does* try hard). The person
who is the biggest help to me is _____
_____ because _____
_____

Look for #105

STACEY THE MATH WHIZ

I had to change my plans before it was too late.

"Ms. Hartley — " I began.

"Oh, I never showed you this!" she interrupted, handing me the computer printout. "The individual scoring totals of every Mathlete in the state — and look who's tied for number one!"

The sheet contained a long list of names and numbers in tiny print. But the top one jumped out at me:

MCGILL, A.

Yes, that's me. (The *A* stands for my full name, Anastasia.) Just below my name, it said SINGH, G., with the same score.

"Apparently, George Singh is a real hotshot in Eastbury," Ms. Hartley explained. "You'll meet him in the finals. Newspaper articles have been written about him. So you can be quite proud of yourself."

Proud? I was flabbergasted! Me, little unknown Stacey, number one math student in the state?

No, *tied* for number one. Which meant I could become number one.

That is, unless I skipped a meet for a concert . . .

Read all the books
about **Abby**
in the Baby-sitters Club series
by Ann M. Martin

The Baby-Sitters Club®

Collect 'em all!

100 (and more)
Reasons to Stay Friends Forever!

More titles... ▶

❏ MG48226-2	#82	Jessi and the Troublemaker	$3.99
❏ MG48235-1	#83	Stacey vs. the BSC	$3.50
❏ MG48228-9	#84	Dawn and the School Spirit War	$3.50
❏ MG48236-X	#85	Claudi Kishi, Live from WSTO	$3.50
❏ MG48227-0	#86	Mary Anne and Camp BSC	$3.50
❏ MG48237-8	#87	Stacey and the Bad Girls	$3.50
❏ MG22872-2	#88	Farewell, Dawn	$3.50
❏ MG22873-0	#89	Kristy and the Dirty Diapers	$3.50
❏ MG22874-9	#90	Welcome to the BSC, Abby	$3.99
❏ MG22875-1	#91	Claudia and the First Thanksgiving	$3.50
❏ MG22876-5	#92	Mallory's Christmas Wish	$3.50
❏ MG22877-3	#93	Mary Anne and the Memory Garden	$3.99
❏ MG22878-1	#94	Stacey McGill, Super Sitter	$3.99
❏ MG22879-X	#95	Kristy + Bart = ?	$3.99
❏ MG22880-3	#96	Abby's Lucky Thirteen	$3.99
❏ MG22881-1	#97	Claudia and the World's Cutest Baby	$3.99
❏ MG22882-X	#98	Dawn and Too Many Sitters	$3.99
❏ MG69205-4	#99	Stacey's Broken Heart	$3.99
❏ MG69206-2	#100	Kristy's Worst Idea	$3.99
❏ MG69207-0	#101	Claudia Kishi, Middle School Dropout	$3.99
❏ MG69208-9	#102	Mary Anne and the Little Princess	$3.99
❏ MG69209-7	#103	Happy Holidays, Jessi	$3.99
❏ MG45575-3		Logan's Story Special Edition Readers' Request	$3.25
❏ MG47118-X		Logan Bruno, Boy Baby-sitter	
		Special Edition Readers' Request	$3.50
❏ MG47756-0		Shannon's Story Special Edition	$3.50
❏ MG47686-6		The Baby-sitters Club Guide to Baby-sitting	$3.25
❏ MG47314-X		The Baby-sitters Club Trivia and Puzzle Fun Book	$2.50
❏ MG48400-1		BSC Portrait Collection: Claudia's Book	$3.50
❏ MG22864-1		BSC Portrait Collection: Dawn's Book	$3.50
❏ MG69181-3		BSC Portrait Collection: Kristy's Book	$3.99
❏ MG22865-X		BSC Portrait Collection: Mary Anne's Book	$3.99
❏ MG48399-4		BSC Portrait Collection: Stacey's Book	$3.50
❏ MG92713-2		The Complete Guide to The Baby-sitters Club	$4.95
❏ MG47151-1		The Baby-sitters Club Chain Letter	$14.95
❏ MG48295-5		The Baby-sitters Club Secret Santa	$14.95
❏ MG45074-3		The Baby-sitters Club Notebook	$2.50
❏ MG44783-1		The Baby-sitters Club Postcard Book	$4.95

Available wherever you buy books...or use this order form.

Scholastic Inc., P.O. Box 7502, 2931 E. McCarty Street, Jefferson City, MO 65102

Please send me the books I have checked above. I am enclosing $_____
(please add $2.00 to cover shipping and handling). Send check or money order–
no cash or C.O.D.s please.

Name_____ Birthdate_____

Address _____

City_____ State/Zip _____

BSC5962

FAN CLUB

Sign up now for a year of great friendships and terrific memories!

★ **110-mm camera!**
   Take photos of your pals!

★ **Mini-photo album**
   Fill it with your best pics!

★ **Diary (with lock!)**
   For your favorite memories...and secret thoughts!

★ **Stationery note cards and stickers**
   Send letters to your far-away friends!

★ **Eight cool pencils**
   With the signatures of different baby-sitters!

★ **Full-color BSC poster**

★ **Subscription to the official BSC newsletter***

★ **Special keepsake shipper**

Amazing stuff!

PHOTOS